GIVE ME LOVE - REASON SERIES #4

Zoey Derrick

GIVE ME LOVE

Zoey Derrick

The entire Reason Series is dedicated to all the men and women around the world who are or have been a victim of Domestic Violence.

ONE

"What have you done to me?" His voice cracks, the effect like gargling gravel. The last thing he knew, he'd come to the cave to tell him about Vivienne. There was a girl with him, but all he can remember is a flash of light and the pain.

The growl comes from across the room. "I have given you life anew! Do not make such inquiries of me again!" From deep in the shadows emerges a man – no, not a man, something far more sinister than anything any man has ever laid eyes upon. Skin the color of charcoal and flame. Two horns at the peak of his skull, and wide, black and red wings even taller than he is flared out behind him.

Understanding immediately that he is once again in the presence of the devil himself, the human kneels in submission. "I'm sorry, my lord."

"Your apologies are weak and unnecessary. A servant of mine does not express remorse." The devil takes two more steps. With each step his body changes, morphing into a body like any other man's. He is tall with long, black hair and deep, dark eyes.

"Rise!" he growls, and the human rises, still looking at the floor. "Look at me."

He raises his head, and shock etches his features. He knows by his voice that the man standing before him is the same demon, but now the demon's features are, well, normal. But the human is not fooled; he knows the demon is still just as menacing as he was a moment ago.

"What I've done to you is bring you back to life." The devil laughs. "I've brought you back because your drive is unparalleled to anything I've ever seen before." He takes another step toward his lesser. "I'm giving you one chance, and one chance only, to bring her to me, dead or alive. If you fail you will spend eternity with the ghouls, who would love nothing more than to torture you after I kill you."

TWO

Mikah has found his own personal heaven on earth: There is nothing sweeter than kissing Vivienne. Her scent is like flowers on a warm summer day. It's heady, and he can't stop himself from kissing her as if his life depends on it.

His hands roam, slowly and gently, up and down her body while his mouth moves along her jaw, down her neck, onto her shoulder. Her head falls back and she squirms under his touch. Her desire for him has grown hotter with each passing touch of his lips. She's never experienced anything so sweet and kind. She understands that what he's doing is proving that she is all that matters, right here, right now.

Her breathing begins to spike as his mouth moves down to her breasts, skirting her nipples. The ache in them is scorching hot and she wants his tongue to ease her need.

Instead, his mouth moves lower still, over her bump to the junction of her thighs. He kisses her there. Licks, and then teasingly drags his teeth along the flesh, and she moans at the sensation. He's yet to make any real contact with any intimate part of her; he's only showing her and her body what he's capable of.

Then his wings blaze at the same time a knock on the door interrupts their heavy breathing. "Mikah. Vivienne. Please, we need to go. Now."

"What? Where?" Mikah moves off of Vivienne, and she instinctively reaches for the covers.

"We need to go into Elysium. Now." Red's voice is stern, unwavering, as Mikah scrambles to his feet.

His eyes meet hers, wary. He wants to explain to her what is going on, but then he sees in her eyes that this is unnecessary; she knows of Elysium and knows more than he thought she knew.

"Mikah, it's alright. Red, give us a moment, please?" She turns her head toward the door but never breaks eye contact with him. "You have nothing to be afraid of. Let's get dressed, okay?" she asks, nodding at him.

Though he's looking at her, he's not entirely sure what he's seeing.

Only a few moments ago they were in the heat of passion. Both their wings have made an appearance, and while he understood then that she knows what he is, he didn't fully understand what he was seeing. Confusion had wracked his brain as he tried hard to decipher whether he was awake or dreaming. But now reality hits him: This is no dream, and she fully knows and understands who and what he is.

He'd noticed when he laid her down that she was without her wings. Asking her seemed like the appropriate thing to do. She'd be his best teacher to show him. "How do I, um…" His voice is gravelly and unsure. "How can I pull these back in?" he manages to finish, and she smiles.

"You concentrate, then visualize them locking back into place. Give it a try."

He steels himself, afraid of what might happen if he isn't able to pull them back in. Then he flexes so that he can feel the point where his wings and body come together.

She watches his wings flare slightly and flap while his face shows that he's concentrating.

Steadily his wings pull in, shrinking moment by moment as he concentrates. Then a furrow appears on his brow, and his wings stop retracting and instead expand.

"Relax, you're doing great," she encourages him.

The furrow softens and he concentrates again. This time he doesn't stop until he feels the click and his wings are locked down.

Opening his eyes, he sees a bright, warm smile on her face. Then his gaze drifts downward and he realizes that she is still topless. The sight of her looking up at him causes his breath to hitch. She really is beautiful; her fair skin, bright red hair, beautiful blue eyes and luscious pink lips drive his desire deeper than it was only a few minutes ago.

The knock on the door comes again, and Vivienne stands and reaches for her shirt. He takes it from her and helps her into it.

She senses his worry, but it's unclear to her whether it is coming from the fear that he thinks she doesn't know about Elysium or if it stems from the fact that Red also seems to know more about what is going on than he does. She tries to ease his worry. "Please Mikah, it will be alright."

He doesn't say anything right away, but he knows deep down that she is right. "I don't have any clothes in here," he says. "Are you good to go in what you're wearing?"

"Yes, I just want to pull my hair back," she says as she slides past him toward the bathroom.

"Don't, I like your hair down."

She smiles and turns toward him.

Tonight they've reached a turning point in their relationship. Everything from here on will be different. That invisible barrier separating them has dropped, and somewhere inside she knows that Mikah is who she wants and what she needs, and that everything is falling into place.

Mikah smiles at her as he heads toward the door. His smile is warm, genuine. That hint of something she's seen before slides over his features again, that something she's yet to figure out but he knows to be love.

He opens the door to find Red standing about two feet away.

"We must hurry," he says, his eyes avoiding Mikah's.

Vivienne comes to stand on the threshold of the bedroom door.

"How is it that you know about Elysium?" Mikah asks. He's not sure he wants to know the answer, but the question will bug him until he knows.

"Mikah," Viv interjects before Red can answer, "I think it is best if we do what he says. I'm sure you can get the answer to that question while we're there."

Mikah strides past Red toward the other bedroom, his body language betraying a mixture of determination and frustration. Vivienne can understand why. He thought he knew all the secrets of those surrounding him, and that is proving to be wrong. Vivienne was the primary secret; he never expected Red to be part of it too.

As Mikah enters the other room, Red says, "Mikah, we will explain everything to you, but right now, we need to go to Elysium."

Vivienne and Red exchange a look. Vivienne starts to follow Mikah, but just before she makes it to the doorway, he comes back out, wearing a black t-shirt and his pajama pants.

"Lead the way," Mikah says.

Red turns and heads back toward the front door, but he stops short at the guest bathroom. He swings open the door to reveal not the expected bathroom but rather the room in Elysium where Vivienne and Mikah have spent so many nights in their dreams.

Mikah stops dead in his tracks. "What the hell is going on here?" he says, confusion radiating off him. The only way he's known how to get into Elysium is through dreams; now all of a sudden his bathroom has been turned into a portal.

Vivienne turns to him and takes a hold of his upper arm. "Mikah, look at me."

He looks at her, his face screwed up with confusion, seeking comfort and explanation.

"It's alright. Let's go do this, and then I will explain everything I know about all of this to you. Okay?" Her voice is sternly sincere.

"Okay," he says, his resolve setting in.

She can see the shift in him as the protector he was born to be returns. She completely understands his reaction; it's similar to her own yesterday morning, when everything she thought she knew was twisted into something else.

He takes her hand from his arm. But rather than brushing her off, he intertwines their fingers, and together they step through the doorway into the white room.

THREE

In front of them is a bank of windows, only this time they can actually see through them into a luscious green garden. In front of them are two couches, one longer and one shorter, that form an L shape around a empty space where a coffee table would normally be.

Off to their right is the outline of another door, only there is no handle or knob to open it. Every other wall in the room is solid white, broken up by small windows.

They come to stand behind the long couch, and on the other side of it is a woman. As they approach, she turns toward them. She is beautiful in a youthful way, with long hair and soft features.

"Hello, Mother," Mikah says with a curt nod in her direction. The tension in his body is visible.

Vivienne recalls that Mikah's mother passed away some years ago, but it is obvious that this isn't the first time he's seen her since then. She wonders why he's so cold toward her.

"My son," she says. "Vivienne, I am Elizabeth," she says and moves a step forward, though she appears to be floating more than walking. "It is an honor to finally meet you." She reaches out her hand and Vivienne steps around the couch to take it. Mikah follows her.

"The same to you," Vivienne says, unsure how to greet her, but Mikah's mother doesn't seem to take any offense.

Elizabeth looks over to Mikah. "It is time for you to learn and to understand all that is going on around you. What I need to tell you is no doubt going to make you angry, but I need you to be calm and listen."

"I cannot make any promises. I'm already upset and confused. How in the world does Red know about all of this?"

Elizabeth's eyebrows shoot up, and she looks at Vivienne with a question in her eyes. Vivienne shakes her head.

"Vivienne?" Mikah says with a hint of menace in his voice.

Vivienne turns toward him. "Maybe you should sit down."

Mikah's eyebrows draw together and his lips purse.

"Don't be mad at me. I've only just learned all of this within the last twenty-four hours or so. Hardly enough time for me to tell you about it."

His features thaw and he takes a seat.

Vivienne lets out a breath, and her shoulders relax.

"Yesterday morning when I woke up, the dream I'd been having filtered into reality, much like it did earlier tonight." She blushes as the memory of Mikah on his knees, his wings spread wide, and the—

She stops the thought but not before she sees his eyes light up with excitement as he too remembers what happened. She blinks, desperate to concentrate.

"When I woke up, I went into the bathroom and caught a glimpse of myself in the mirror and I almost screamed. Once I began to realize what had happened, Zirah, my teacher—" His eyes snap up to hers; he, too, has a teacher. "—came to me and explained what had happened and how to fix it. She also told me that those closest to us are our greatest allies and protectors. Red—" She gestures behind Mikah to the man standing behind him. "—Andrew, Connor and Celeste are all guardians of Elysium." She pauses to give him a moment soak up the information she's giving him.

While he processes it, Vivienne, too, is struck by how strange this all sounds. Now that she hears herself say it aloud, the thought that none of this is real flits through her mind.

"How... Why?" he says.

Vivienne turns toward Elizabeth.

"When you chose the business path you did, you put yourself in the public eye. I had no choice but to help protect you, not only from evil, but from yourself." Elizabeth starts to pace. "When I died, Shannon knew nothing of angels, knew nothing of what you were or were to become, so the stories stopped with me. We feared that, should your inner angel make himself known, we would be exposed to the world. But it would also expose you to the demons who wish to harm you." Elizabeth continues to pace. "Demons seek out angels on Earth to either destroy them or convert them."

Mikah has a flash of intuition that this information is important, but before he can ask about it, Elizabeth goes on. "When you started looking for bodyguards, we sent Red in. Then the rest of your staff. Andrew and Connor are just as he is, and Celeste too."

Elizabeth continues to pace around the room. Viv looks to Mikah, who is sitting still as can be, his head in his hands. The tension in his shoulders could shatter a boulder to a million pieces. This is not what he was expecting to hear tonight.

"Mikah?" Vivienne says quietly as she comes to stand next to him. Looking down at him, she sees his shoulders relax and the tension wash out of him. He lazily raises his head, and when their eyes meet, everything seems to stop. Nothing matters but him. She senses that need he feels for her, and her heart swells.

Their connection is broken by a clicking sound, like a door closing behind Vivienne, and she turns quickly in that direction. A momentary fear causes her heart to start racing. Striding toward them are two women more beautiful than anything Vivienne has ever seen before. The woman in front is blond with hair that flows out behind her. The second one is red-haired and fair-skinned, much like Vivienne. They wear matching white dresses befitting Grecian goddesses.

The red-haired one smiles at Vivienne, who takes an involuntary step back. "Do not be frightened," she says, bells for a voice, and Vivienne immediately recognizes her.

"Zirah?" Vivienne asks. The redhead nods enthusiastically at her, and a warm smile spreads across Vivienne's face. Vivienne feels Mikah move behind her, and her eyes go to the blond woman, whose face lights up.

"Hello, Mikah," the blond woman says. "I am Seraphina."

Though he doesn't smile back at her, Mikah's eyes register recognition. "Hello, Seraphina."

Once again there is a click behind them, this time from the door they'd entered through a few minutes ago. Mikah and Vivienne watch as Zirah and Seraphina quickly look past Mikah and Vivienne toward the noise.

Standing in front of the door are Andrew, who is smiling of course; Connor, who looks pissed off as usual; and Celeste, who gives her usual impression of Mexican jumping beans bouncing around inside their shell.

"Now that we're all here it is time to discuss the real reasons I've called on you. Vivienne, I have some rather sad news to share with you. Your mother—"

Vivienne's ears begin to ring, and she does not need to hear more to know that Elizabeth is trying to tell her that her mother has passed away. Her body goes limp, but Mikah catches her quickly and carries her to the sofa.

"Vivienne." Elizabeth tries again to gather her attention. "Vivienne, your mother, Rebecca, did not die of natural causes."

"What?" Mikah and Vivienne say in unison, his more of a growl.

"How?" is all Vivienne can manage to say, but then she realizes she already knows the answer to that question. He's back.

"Riley."

FOUR

"I always knew that little shit wasn't done," Mikah snaps.

Vivienne's body begins to shake with silent sobs, and Mikah does the only thing he thinks he can do to console her: He gently strokes her hair. She leans deeper into him. Her gesture is silent assurance that she needs him as much as he needs her.

Vivienne always knew that this day would come, but she never expected it to come at the hands of Riley Bennett. Vivienne had been sure that Riley knew nothing of her mother. In fact, he never so much as showed an inkling of interest in her. So how had he found her?

"We're not entirely sure it was Riley," Elizabeth says, and Vivienne and Mikah both look up at her.

"How are you not sure?" Mikah asks the question that Vivienne can't.

"Well, we simply haven't had the time to investigate what happened, and Rebecca has been no help."

"What do you mean?" Vivienne asks. Her voice is full of emotion and the words are hard to understand.

"We mean yes, we suspect as much, but we are unable to confirm it just yet. We have a small team on their way to investigate and report back," Elizabeth is quick to answer.

"But you said something about Rebecca being of no help," Vivienne says, a little clearer now.

"We've brought Rebecca to Elysium."

"She's here?" Vivienne and Mikah both say at the same time in nearly identical flat tones. They both look to each other.

Mikah can see the fear in her eyes, and he squeezes her hand slightly, just to let her know that he's here for her no matter what.

"Yes, she's here and we're trying to talk to her. However, it takes some time for the departed to adjust to what's happened, and I'm afraid she hasn't been much help." Elizabeth begins to pace back and forth again in front of the bank of windows near the couches. "We also have to take into account the fact that your mother was not of sound mind prior to her death. We're not sure if we will get any information from her at all. But we're going to try."

There is a moment of silence while this news sinks in, and then Elizabeth stops pacing and speaks again. "Vivienne," she says, "I'm wondering if you could help us?"

Vivienne looks to Elizabeth, a quizzical look on her face. "I'm not sure what help I can be," she says finally.

Mikah leans in a little, curious as to what his mother is asking.

"I'm wondering if you would try talking to your mother, see if she will tell you what she knows about her death."

"Elizabeth, I—" Vivienne looks to Mikah, confusion on her face, and then back to Elizabeth. "I don't think that's a good idea."

Mikah looks to Vivienne, trying to read her reaction, but he can't. Too many emotions are playing out on her features.

"I think it might be the best chance we have to get her to talk."

"I'm pretty sure that won't work." Vivienne's heart is pounding, making it impossible to think straight. Nothing good can come from seeing Rebecca, at least not anything that won't result in more heartache.

"Vivienne, we should at least try," Elizabeth says.

Mikah moves to stand behind Vivienne and places his hand on the small of her back. He leans down and whispers in her ear, "You can do this."

It's strange how his words have calmed her almost instantly.

Vivienne smiles slightly, takes a deep breath and says, "Bring her here."

FIVE

Two heartbeats later, the door behind Zirah and Seraphina clicks again. Zirah and Seraphina part, allowing Vivienne a full view of the woman who has just entered the room.

Vivienne feels trepidation fly through her veins. She stands and takes a few steps toward the woman. Mikah is close behind her; she can hear the shifting and footsteps.

The woman is modestly dressed in a white nightgown-style, sleeveless dress and has long reddish-brown hair framing her heart-shaped face. Her green eyes stare wary at the scene laid out in front of her, but she is doing her best to pretend she's not looking. Though the woman looks lost and confused, it doesn't take but a few moments for Vivienne to recognize her.

"Rebecca?" Vivienne says, and the woman, who is the focus of the entire room, jerks her head in Vivienne's direction. Vivienne knows it's her mother, but the woman before her appears much younger, as if she is about Vivienne's age.

The woman looks at Vivienne, her eyes squinting for a moment before widening as she realizes who she's looking at. "Vivienne?" She takes a few steps toward Vivienne.

Vivienne takes a step back. She realizes now she wasn't ready for this. Needing support and reassurance, she tears her gaze away from the her mother and turns to see Mikah right next to her. She feels oddly comforted by his look of confusion. Behind him, the same look is on the faces of her guardians and she can sense their tension.

Mikah isn't entirely sure what to say or how to interpret what he is looking at. He'd expected an older woman.

"Is that...?" Mikah says aloud.

"Rebecca, Vivienne's mother," Elizabeth answers.

Mikah hears a sharp intake of breath behind him and looks over his shoulder to see Red, who is white as a ghost. Mikah follows Red's gaze back to the woman standing in front of them. She appears dazed, obviously in shock.

"Vivienne?" the woman says again, and Viv takes another step back toward the line of people standing behind her.

Mikah cocks his head, trying to understand how this woman, who is no older than Vivienne, could be her mother.

Elizabeth answers his unasked question. "When those who die on earth are brought to Elysium, they take on the appearance of their younger selves, when they were happiest and when they were their healthiest."

Behind Mikah, Red has started mumbling to himself. Mikah turns his head to look, and his forehead creases in confusion. Red is staring intently at Vivienne's mother as if he knows her. Mikah strains to hear what he is saying, but it's incomprehensible.

"What is going on here?" Mikah says.

Vivienne looks at him, confused, but then her gaze follows his to Red, and Red's back to Rebecca, who is still staring at Vivienne.

"Red?" Mikah says, watching Rebecca closely.

She doesn't disappoint him. She raises her eyes to Mikah, and then her gaze shifts from Mikah to the man standing to his right.

Vivienne takes a few more steps backwards, putting distance between herself and everyone else. She can't stop staring at Red.

"I always thought there was something strangely familiar about you," Vivienne says, "but I could never place it. The picture. The one I carry in my purse." Vivienne looks from Red to her mother and back again. "It's you in that picture, isn't it?"

"Vivienne, what are you talking about?" Mikah says.

He takes a step toward her, and she steps away from him. He reaches out for her, but she doesn't see it. She's still staring at Red.

"You—" She squints and cocks her head to the side. Red squints back at her and there is no doubt in her mind. "You're my father."

SIX

Red can only stare at Vivienne, looking confused. Something is passing between them when someone breaks the silence within the room.

"Impossible," Seraphina says. Her voice isn't angry, but rather sweet and breathless.

"Vivienne, I—" Red stops. Something in his voice and the way he is looking at Vivienne suggest that he had no idea.

Suddenly Vivienne understands. "Mother, is there something you'd like to tell us all?" she says sternly.

"Yes, please do." This time it's Mikah.

Vivienne finally pulls her eyes away from Red to look at Mikah. The concern is clear on his features, but his eyes are alight with curiosity, too, as this twenty-two year old mystery unfolds.

"I...I don't know," Rebecca says, but Vivienne isn't fooled. Her mother is notorious for avoiding the truth.

Vivienne turns toward her mother, who is still staring at Red. "For the love of Christ, Mother, now is not the time for games or jokes." The wings on Vivienne's back flare in frustration. "This is it, isn't it? Despite the fact that you're here, you're still going to continue to play games. Stop it. I've had enough. Is he or is he not my father?"

Rebecca starts to sob, and she crumples, as if in pain, to the floor.

Andrew and Connor rush to help her, but Vivienne puts her hand up. "Stop, leave her be. She's still up to her same old tricks. Resorting to tears to get her way or avoid dealing with something she knows she needs to explain. She doesn't want to discuss this, so she is going to play the blubbering fool on the floor." Vivienne notices Mikah out of the corner of her eye. He is gaping at her, slack-jawed, and she realizes he's never seen her like this.

Vivienne is also surprised by her tone. Growing up, she could never be cross with her mother. But now, after all this time, the anger and frustration have reached a boiling point, and she resolves to be done with her mother's games.

"Red?" Mikah says.

"I honestly don't know. I met Rebecca some years ago, and—" He stops again.

Vivienne looks toward him. He seems to be doing some math in his head.

"It would've been about twenty-three years ago. I was pulled away, brought back to Elysium by—" He looks toward Elizabeth. "—Alexandria. About the time Mikah's wings were discovered."

"Wait, what do my wings have to do with— I've only known you for a few years." Mikah looks to his mother for an explanation.

But it's Red who answers. "No, I've known you since you were a lad, since shortly after your family came to Boston. Though neither you nor your mother ever saw me, I was sent to keep watch over you. To protect you."

As Red talks he is trying desperately to understand and put all the pieces of this together. "As I said, I was pulled away from Rebecca by Alexandria, who was dethroned to make way for you, Elizabeth. She told me that I was to stay away from Rebecca, that I could never return. I questioned her, but she wouldn't explain it to me. Then I met Kelly. Though I never truly forgot Rebecca, I was — and am — so taken with Kelly that I never regretted the way things turned out."

Vivienne's eyes scan the room, unseeing, as she tries to understand everything that Red is saying. There is a connection here, something between Elizabeth, Red, Alexandria, and herself that she doesn't understand.

"I was pulled away in late February. That would have been twenty-two years ago." Red looks to Rebecca. "Were you pregnant when I left? Were you pregnant with Vivienne?" he asks, his voice low.

"Yes." Rebecca sobs, still kneeling on the tile with her head in her hands.

An eerie silence follows, finally broken by Mikah addressing Elizabeth. "Mother, did you know about all of this?"

"Yes and no. I knew that Vivienne's father was of angelic descent, I just didn't have the details. Our archives are incomplete or missing," Elizabeth says, and she doesn't elaborate further.

SEVEN

"Rebecca," Vivienne says, her voice strong and determined. She's finally recalled the reason Elizabeth brought Rebecca here, and she's going to get answers.

Her mother looks up at her, tears still streaming down her cheeks.

"We need to ask you a few questions." Despite the fact that every muscle in her body is tight and her hands are shaking, Vivienne's voice sounds confident. She feels Mikah's hand on her back and she relaxes just a little bit more.

"I need to ask you about what happened tonight."

Everyone in the room takes an added interest in Rebecca and what she has to say, but Rebecca's face only shows confusion.

"Uh..." Rebecca's features goes through a series of different emotions: confusion, concern, thoughtfulness. Finally she says, "The last thing I remember is hearing a girl scream."

"Girl scream?" Vivienne repeats. Now the same puzzled look on Rebecca's features is displayed on Vivienne's.

"Yes, and there was a lot of noise – fighting or arguing – then a loud crack and a door slamming shut." She pauses, thinking harder about what she remembers. "There was a man. He was pushing her around, but I couldn't see him. I was sitting on a couch. After the door slammed shut, I heard scraping noises and then pounding."

Vivienne begins to shake uncontrollably. As her knees give out, Mikah is quick to catch her. Her heart is beating harder and faster than anything she's felt in a long time. Her breathing becomes quick and shallow.

"The man comes to me. He's dressed in blue jeans. He's taking off—"

"Enough," Mikah snaps, and Rebecca falls silent. "Vivienne, look at me. You're safe, no one can hurt you." He brushes a few stray strands of hair out of her face. She's clearly petrified, scared out of her mind, but Mikah can't even begin to understand where this is coming from.

Vivienne's heart rate is slowing, little by little. With each passing beat the memory begins to fade away and she can feel her strength returning.

"Vivienne," says a sweet, soft voice a little distance away. Vivienne recognizes it as Zirah's, but she can't turn away from Mikah to look at her. The sadness in his heart can be seen through his eyes.

"That wasn't a memory of what happened to her tonight," Vivienne whispers to Mikah.

"What is she talking about then?" he says back to her, wishing he knew how to comfort Vivienne in this moment.

Vivienne moves to sit up, stand up, and Mikah doesn't hold her back. She gets back to her feet, wobbling a bit, but Mikah is there to support her.

"She's talking about a night that happened nearly seven years ago."

Rebecca is trying to understand what Vivienne is saying, but she can't seem to remember anything.

"She's talking," Vivienne says, "about what happened the night she had her stroke. When I was locked in the closet for three days." She turns to her mother, eyes flashing. "Three days until the police showed up," Vivienne says, glaring at Rebecca. "The last night that you stood by while your *pimp*—" The word drips with anger and pain. "—beat me and locked me away so that he could do whatever it was he wanted to do."

No one in the room says a word, unsure of what to say, including Mikah. He knows that she needs to say what she needs to say and he can't stop her.

"Vivienne, I—" Rebecca says. The look on her face says more than her words can; she is scared and unsure.

"Don't," Vivienne snaps. "You have no idea what you've put me through, nothing you say now will change that." Everyone can see how her words cut into Rebecca, but Vivienne doesn't want to hear her apologies. "I need to know if you remember anything at all from *last night.*"

Rebecca tries to think, tries to remember, but she's so confused. She comes up empty. "I don't remember."

EIGHT

"What are we supposed to do now?" Mikah says after Seraphina and Zirah have escorted Rebecca out and come back to stand with the group once again.

Surprisingly, it is Red who steps forward. "You were about to receive a call from the rehab center. We believe the phone call was meant to be a trap to lure Vivienne to whoever killed her mother."

"Okay, so we don't go to the funeral home. Got it. Now what?" The irritation in Mikah's voice is heard by all. The secrets and the vague descriptions and explanations are really starting to piss him off.

"Do not take that tone."

"What do you expect me to do, Mother? You've thrown all of this at us at lightning speed. I will not sit here idly as everything Vivienne's ever known begins to crumble." His statement would've been more effectively delivered if he'd been standing, but the second he started speaking, Vivienne's arms had wrapped harder and tighter around him, reminding him that she was there with him. "I need to know what I need to do to stop that madman from—"

The look on Elizabeth's face forces him to stop talking.

"If it was that madman, as you call him, then you need to know that he has become the left hand of the devil himself. He was brought out of whatever circle of hell he was in to come after her. Though it is not truly Vivienne that he is after. It is her child."

Mikah's heart pounds hard against his ribs, and Vivienne's head jerks off his chest. They both stare at Elizabeth.

"What does he want with my baby?" Her voice cracks with a strength of emotion unlike anything Mikah's ever heard from her before. It's that deep-seated level of emotion only a mother could express. Mikah has heard it many times from his own mother.

"Riley's initial attack on you, when you told him you were pregnant, was driven by vengeance. But when he did that, the devil saw in him something he could use: a weapon of hatred that could be used to destroy that which could destroy the devil himself." Elizabeth looks at both of them with worry and sadness in her eyes, but lying underneath is something else, something that Mikah doesn't quite understand.

"Go ahead, explain all of this," Mikah says sternly.

"Vivienne is the sole remaining descendant of *Dia.*"

"What? How?" he whispers.

Vivienne looks to him in confusion.

"Those stories are long and better told by a *scéalaí,*" Elizabeth says, "though they are very hard to find. Alexandria, the matron who preceded me, was dethroned because she refused to relinquish the location of *Dia's* heir. She believed that if no one knew of Vivienne's existence then Vivienne would always remain safe. But

Dia knew that in order to protect his heir, we all needed to know where she was."

Mikah and Vivienne's eyes meet. But Elizabeth doesn't pause for questions.

"For thousands of years we've believed that a full-blooded angel could only be male, as there were no records of females of full-blooded ancestry."

"What about you?" Mikah asks. "Given your position within Elysium."

"One would assume, but no. I am only half angel. Your father, on the other hand, is full-blooded." She pauses momentarily, but Mikah doesn't feel it's appropriate to take the opportunity to ask about his birth father. Elizabeth continues, "Vivienne's mother is the closest thing to a full-blooded female that Alexandria knew of. When Rebecca met Vivienne's father—" A strange look crosses Elizabeth's face and there is some uncomfortable shifting around the room. Vivienne shifts in her seat and starts to play with her fingers. "—Red, who is also full-blooded, and they conceived Vivienne, she became the next closest pureblood. Even so, Vivienne is only about fifteen-sixteenths angel."

Vivienne's hand gently caresses the swell of her stomach, finally understanding the importance of her baby.

"Yes, my child. Your daughter is of the purest angelic blood that we know of, and possibly the closest we will ever come to a full-blooded female."

Vivienne opens her mouth to say something, but words fail her, and Elizabeth drives home what Vivienne already knows.

"Riley too is a full-blood. He, however, is of the demonic bloodline."

"SHIT!" Mikah exclaims.

NINE

Seraphina is quick to speak. "Calm down, Mikah, this doesn't mean anything is wrong. We have several angels here in Elysium that have more demonic blood than angelic. Just because demon blood runs in their veins does not make them a demon."

Mikah looks to Vivienne, who has a wary look in her eyes.

Though Vivienne's heart rate spikes at the confirmation that Riley is of demonic descent, it is also something she's suspected since all of this angel stuff was brought into her life.

"Vivienne." Zirah is vying for her attention. Vivienne pulls her eyes away from Mikah to look at her. "Your daughter will be full-blooded angel. There is nothing in this world that could pull her away from that path."

"How can you be so certain?" Vivienne breathes.

This time Elizabeth is the one to speak. "Why, child, would she be anything but? She will be taught our ways, live amongst the purest of angels. She will know no different. Take a look at your life, Vivienne. You've dealt with far more than any one person should have to endure in a normal lifetime, and look at yourself, what you've turned into. You've never followed the path of evil, why would your daughter?"

Though Elizabeth sounds confident, it is hard for Vivienne or Mikah to be certain of the path her daughter will take.

"Some of the devil's demons are full-blooded angel, as well," Zirah says. "The path we choose dictates where we will spend our lives. Those who choose the path of evil stay evil, and those who choose the path of good stay good. Their goodness or evil is heightened by their blood, but their blood does not dictate their path."

Vivienne is trying to process Zirah's words.

"Take your mother for example, and we've already talked about this, but while she never did anything to earn herself a spot in hell, she's done enough away from the good that she cannot live in Elysium and is considered one of our fallen."

The reality of her mother's banishment from Elysium is slowly starting to sink in. Vivienne wipes tears away from her cheeks as Mikah softly rubs his thumb along her back. She wonders if she'll ever see her mother again.

When you're ready to see her again, we can bring her back here, Zirah says quietly inside her mind.

Vivienne looks to Zirah. Vivienne's heart rate spikes, she fights the urge to let the revulsion play out on her face.

Only when you're ready.

Vivienne realizes she doesn't know if she'll ever be ready to face her mother again. Suddenly she feels overwhelmed by everything that's happened in the last several hours, and exhaustion overtakes her.

Mikah senses a shift in Vivienne. His ability to feel and read her emotions has him sliding closer to her.

"I'm not sure how much more of tonight I can take," Vivienne whispers, and Mikah wraps his arms around her.

The guardians exchange urgent glances with Elizabeth, silently pleading with her to let them all go for tonight.

"Go and rest. We will have more information soon, and when we do, I'll bring you back here," Elizabeth says.

Vivienne leans into Mikah, and the rest of the guardians are quick to lead them to an exit.

When they walk back through the door, they are no longer in Vivienne's condo, but in Mikah's.

"Until we know what's going on, I think it would be best if you both stayed here," Red says as he turns back toward Vivienne and Mikah.

Vivienne nods, and Mikah holds her a little tighter.

"Thank you," Mikah says.

Red nods at him, but his eyes fall to Vivienne. She can see the sadness in his eyes.

"Vivienne, I—" But he falters. Red, usually so sure of himself, is at a loss for words.

Vivienne breathes. "It's a lot to take in. I'm exhausted. Can we talk about this later?"

Red's lips form a half smile. "Of course. Get some rest. I'll come if there is news."

"Please wait until at least tomorrow afternoon, no matter how urgent you think it might be," Mikah says.

Red nods, and he and the others leave.

TEN

"How are you?" Mikah asks as soon as they are alone.

"Tired, scared, concerned, tired, confused. What about you?" she asks as she leans into him.

He gently kisses the top of her forehead. "All of the above. Let's go to bed."

They both start toward the bedroom. "Are you okay with staying here?" he asks her, knowing how she feels about her independence and not wanting to upset her by forcing her to stay.

"I'm happy to be wherever you are."

Mikah's heart swells at her words and he stops, gently taking her cheeks in his hand, and kisses her, softly and tenderly.

She returns his kiss, this time without any hesitation. Knowing that tonight they've crossed a line that can never be recrossed, she puts everything she feels into their kiss.

Mikah pulls back and looks deep into her eyes. She recognizes that underlying emotion. Similar emotions are running wild through her veins, she takes his hand and he leads her into the bedroom.

As she steps across the threshold, the dream image of her and Mikah in this bed comes back into her mind, and she's reminded of how ready she is for their relationship to move forward.

"I'm going to use the bathroom," she says as she heads in that direction.

Once inside, she takes stock of herself in the mirror, runs water over her face and tries to take a deep breath. She doesn't understand why she's suddenly so nervous.

When she steps back into the bedroom, Mikah is standing on the opposite side of the bed, pulling back the covers.

He looks up to see her standing in the doorway. A brief moment passes between them, and then he gestures for her to come to him.

He watches her as she walks quietly around the bed. Her hair bounces across her back, and she smiles at him as she comes closer. The desire he felt for her earlier tonight grows deeper within him and he wants her. After all the mess in Elysium, he needs her close to him.

He reaches for her hand and gestures toward the bed, and she takes her cue and climbs in. He bends down and kisses her forehead.

"I'll be right back," he whispers as he steps back and goes around the bed toward the bathroom.

Vivienne snuggles into bed, turning to face the other side, where she expects Mikah to lie down when he returns.

While she waits for him, her mind begins to go over everything that has happened in the last twenty-four hours: the shifter in her apartment; learning about who and what Red, Connor, Andrew and Celeste are; the news of her mother's passing; the new information about Riley. She has no doubt that he is behind her mother's death, and she wonders how much more destruction he will create in his haste to get to her. And then her confrontation with her mother and the discovery of who her father is.

What is she supposed to do about Red? Is she capable, after all this time, of embracing that relationship? What will Red think if she doesn't know what to do?

"Easy," she whispers to herself. "You can deal with that tomorrow."

Just then Mikah steps out of the bathroom. He's wearing the same pants, but he's shed his shirt. Seeing Mikah standing there shirtless, his inky black hair falling onto his face and those liquid eyes vibrant and blue, has her desire for him growing hot and fast throughout her veins.

Vivienne's beautiful. Her soft cheeks are flushed, and a hint of a smile plays on her lips. Seeing her in his bed brings back the memory of seeing her with his other self in that dream so many weeks ago.

He'd wanted to stop earlier, unsure of what she was really feeling for him, but seeing her now leaves no doubt in his mind that they are both on the same page, both wanting and needing each other in a way he's never felt before.

But he won't push it. She needs to come to him when she's ready.

Resolving to be patient, he walks the ten steps to the bed. As he does, she pulls the covers back to receive him. Excitement spreads like wildfire through his veins. Just the idea of sleeping in the same bed as her is enough to send his heart racing.

But his mind is running wild with what happened earlier tonight and everything that's happened between them in just the last few hours. He needs a chance to collect himself and bring his overwhelming need for her under control.

She watches as he turns to sit down on the edge of the bed. He puts his elbows on his knees and rubs his face. She reaches over and lightly runs her fingers down his back along his wings.

He shivers with pleasure at her touch, and he can feel his wings unlocking themselves. Closing his eyes, he hopes to keep them in check. She does it again and he turns toward her.

She's so beautiful, unlike anything he's ever seen before. He can no longer resist; he climbs into bed facing her.

"Hi, beautiful," he whispers.

She slides closer to him, brushing his hair out of his eyes. He kisses her palm and she shivers.

He wraps his arms around her, holding her close, trying to understand her mood, or her need. Having her close to him, knowing that she's safe in his arms, helps to bring his racing heart back to normal.

Relief washes through Vivienne as she settles into his embrace and feels his heartbeat slow. While being with Mikah is what she wants more than anything, she's too tired.

Before they can even consider anything further, exhaustion claims them and they both fall sound asleep.

ELEVEN

"Your plan isn't working. We have to get out of here before we get caught."

"No. We wait for her."

"Why, she's not showing up here. You said it yourself, you never even knew she had a mother until Link told you. If her mother didn't mean enough to her to tell you, what makes you think she will show up here?"

Riley turns away from the window in Rebecca Callahan's old room. He looks the same as he did before the devil killed him in that cave, but he's far more powerful now. "I just know," he snaps. He runs his hand across his buzz cut hair and looks back to the window

Derek, the idiot Link made him bring along, has been pacing the floor on the other side of the bed since they got here. Riley's six-foot-one frame is big enough, but Derek dwarfs him. His military-short hair is jet black, and his features are hard. His eyes are a solid black, something Riley guesses he's gained from all his years of service to Link. Derek is also someone Link trusts, otherwise he wouldn't be here now. Link had made Riley fight Derek before he left hell, and the idiot had somehow managed to kick his ass. The last thing Riley wants to do is admit Derek might be right, that Vivienne might not come after all.

He'd succeeded in taking care of Rebecca so that no one would think she'd died of anything other than natural causes. Then he'd read her chart. Vivienne, no doubt, drove her to the madness she suffered from. Vivienne isn't good for anything other than pissing everyone off.

"I wouldn't be too sure about that. Let's go."

"You go then, if you're so damn concerned about the humans."

"Let me explain something to you, Riley. You don't call the shots here, he does. You will follow orders or you will end up back where he pulled you from. You get me?"

Riley shivers at the memory of hell. He vowed to complete his task just so he wouldn't have to return to the pits he was pulled from. Anything is better than being sliced open and left to bleed out, only to heal back up and go through it all over again.

All Riley wants to do is be done with this mess. He could've sworn up and down that when he'd left Vivienne in her apartment she wasn't breathing and didn't have a pulse. Once this is over, Link will see that he means business and let him keep working for him and, more importantly, let him keep working with the amazing powers the devil himself has given him.

"Fine," Riley spats finally. "I'm going to see my father."

"I wouldn't do that if I were you," Derek says as they leave the room.

They walk down the hallway toward the exit door at the end of the hall. It has a warning on it that an alarm will sound when opened, but they crash the bar and go right through, and no alarm goes off.

"What the fuck do you care?"

"The cops are watching your dad's place."

"What do I care about cops?"

Derek slams him up against the brick wall of the building they've just left. "You better start caring. If you fuck this up, get caught or get yourself killed, you will be tortured, and believe me, you don't want to have to deal with that again."

But Riley shoves him off, straightens his jacket, and takes off as fast as he can toward his father's house.

TWELVE

A few hours later, Vivienne stirs in his arms. Opening her eyes, she can see that it is still early; it's very dark in the room. Unsure of what woke her, she snuggles closer to Mikah.

This isn't the first time she's woken up next to him, but this is the first time since she came to understand all the hidden emotions she's been fighting. She squirms slightly and he stirs.

"What's wrong?" he asks, and she can hear the concern in his voice.

"Nothing, I just woke up. That's all."

"Oh."

She pulls herself closer to him, pressing their bodies tighter together. She can't stop what happens next; it comes so natural to her now. She leans in and softly places her lips to his.

Her heart begins to race, desire shattering the nerves that have built up since they stepped into the room. Last night, seeing him on the floor on his knees with his wings extended had brought out her deepest desires for him, ones that were, at one time, only felt in their dreams, and she couldn't stop herself.

She can't stop herself now.

He kisses her back, letting go of all his inhibitions, and he lets her take the lead.

She hitches her leg onto his hip and pushes him onto his back. Rolling with him, she now sits atop him, her hands sliding down his cheeks, down his neck. Their kisses grow more and more passionate with every touch.

She runs her hands down his chest and back up to his shoulders, then down along his arms until she finds his hands. She lifts them to her body, encouraging him to touch, to explore, and he takes the not-so-subtle hint.

While their soft, warm tongues continue dancing, he ever so lightly runs his hands from her hips up her sides and down her arms. Her desire for him skyrockets to a fever pitch.

She shivers, and that need she feels for him grows hotter, stronger, making her bold and brave. This is it. This is what she's been needing: to know that she can have him as completely as he has her.

Until a moment ago, kissing Mikah was all she could think about, all she ever wanted to do, and she wants more. She trails her fingers down his chest and over his abs, lightly tracing the bumps with her fingertips until they reach the point where their bodies meet. She can feel it between them, his erection growing stronger.

His hands glide down her body once again, but she longs to feel his fingers against her bare skin. She grabs the hem of her shirt.

His hands cover hers, stopping them. Through their kiss he whispers, "Are you sure?"

"Yes," she breathes back, and he lets go of her hands.

"Can I?" he whispers again, and she nods.

At a slow, measured pace, he pulls the hem of her shirt up. Once the t-shirt rises higher than her breasts, the cool air of the room hardens her nipples into tight, painful peaks, and desire explodes. It causes her wings to unlock and spread.

She raises her arms to allow the shirt to come off, but in order for it to come off, she has to stop kissing him. She doesn't want to stop kissing him.

Mikah pulls away from their kiss long enough to bring the neckline of her shirt over her mouth. Then he is instantly kissing her again. He stops pulling on the shirt, but it still covers her eyes. She smiles as she kisses him again; she's trapped slightly by her shirt.

His hands are on her bare skin, leaving goose bumps in their wake. She shivers again and her wings rustle. She pulls her shirt off the rest of the way, and as soon as she tosses it aside she hears Mikah's sharp intake of breath. His touch radiates through her wings and is felt deep down there. She moans into his mouth.

"You're so beautiful," he breathes as his hands continue their exploration.

He sits up, taking her with him so they are nose to nose, lips against lips. His hands slide up her sides to the swell of her breasts, tickling along her heated skin until his fingers brush her nipples and she moans again.

He pulls his lips away from hers and begins to kiss along her jaw, down her neck. Vivienne is lost to his touch; nothing matters but the two of them. His mouth continues down her chest to her breast — licking, kissing, nipping lightly as she writhes in his lap — until finally his tongue makes brief, searing contact with her nipple and she trembles.

He feels the tremor along the shaft of his throbbing erection, and suddenly he's on the verge of losing control.

Sensing his distress and pleasure, she flicks her hips against his erection once again. This time he responds by running his hand along the front part of her wing. She stops as the pleasure locks down all of her muscles in a delicious tease. The moment his hand comes away, she is released.

"Not fair," she says.

She smiles and breathes. Bringing her own hands around to his back, she brushes her fingers along the edges of his wings, which are still locked away, but the touch has the same effect: He is locked down with desire.

He turns, pushing her onto the bed, but before she makes contact, her wings disappear. He laughs at how quickly she pulled them back in.

"Now it's my turn," he says.

He slides his body between her legs and she wraps them around his hips, holding him tight. He kisses her again, then slowly licks and kisses his way down her body, between her breasts, and further still. Her legs fall slack and she runs her hands through his hair, urging him to keep going.

His lips come to the top of her bump, and he kisses it ever so tenderly. She fights the urge to cry as the emotions swell inside her. Something deeper spreads within her, a feeling she's never experienced before and never wants to lose, as he softly kisses her belly along the waistband of her yoga pants.

He's never felt this way about anyone before – at once nearly overwhelmed by his desire for her but also desperately needing to take things slow.

His hands slide into the waistband of her pants, and she responds by lifting her hips so that he can remove them. But he doesn't pull them off immediately. Instead he continues to kiss along the lower swell of her belly.

"I will always protect you," he says, his lips brushing against her belly while his eyes never waver from hers.

She knows that his declaration is not just for her, but is for her daughter too. All the raw emotion boils over, and this time she can't hold back the tears.

THIRTEEN

"I will always be here for you," he breathes against her belly. "Never doubt that." He can feel her emotion pouring into him. It is the emotion that he needs to feel in order to continue.

Vivienne is not just a girl in his bed; she is the woman who has his heart. Her emotions tell him that he has hers and lets him know that what he's been fighting for for weeks is finally going to be his.

In agonizingly slow fashion, he begins to slide her pants down her legs. She doesn't stop him. She needs this. She needs him. She fought for so long to prove to herself that she needed nothing and no one, but right now, she realizes that she was wrong. She needs him like she needs air to breathe.

As he's freeing her legs, he can't stop his eyes from wondering up her beautiful body. He slowly moves up her body, sliding his hands along her legs to her hips, and he watches as she closes her eyes to savor the sensations. He needs to worship her body, show her what she means to him.

She senses his need as he gets closer to her lips. He pauses to flick his tongue across one nipple, then the other, and she moans with each contact. Then finally he reaches her lips.

Throwing aside all resistance, he kisses her with more passion than he's ever felt in his entire life.

She wraps her arms around him and pulls him against her as tight as she can, needing to feel his skin on hers.

Using her feet, she tries to push down his pants. He smiles, knowing that she wants what he wants just as badly. He pulls back from their kiss and rears up, which allows him to slide his pants down his legs. She surprises him by maintaining eye contact; he can't pull his eyes away from hers.

He manages to liberate his raging erection from the constraint of his pants. Then he leans back down and kisses her once again.

She wraps her legs around him again, holding him to her. She can feel his erection pressed against her pelvic bone, so close, and her growing need for him can be felt in the warm wetness between her legs.

When his erection makes contact with that wetness, he cannot hold back anymore. "Are you sure?" he breathes against her lips, needing her reassurance.

"I've never been more ready for anything than I am right now."

That's all he needs to hear. He pulls his hips back, lining up the head of his erection with the warmth of her sex.

"Please," she breathes, and slowly he pushes into her.

She can feel her body giving way to his sensual invasion, feel when the crown makes it past the tightness of her entrance. He's bigger than anything she's ever felt before.

He moves unhurriedly, not wanting to hurt her, knowing that he is larger than most men. Vivienne writhes beneath him as he pushes himself inside.

Vivienne has never felt anything like this before. Her body is stretching and contracting in ways she's never experienced. Just when she thinks she can't take anymore, he pushes in a little deeper, filling her a little fuller.

He finally stops pushing when he feels significant resistance. He pauses, looking deep into her eyes, waiting patiently for her to adjust to him inside of her. When she starts to move, he takes it as his cue that she's ready.

He pulls back and then slides in a little faster. The pleasure within her starts to fire through her veins like lightning. His hands roam her body from her hips to her belly to her breasts. Her eyes close, the better to feel his touch and savor the sensations flying through her body. She moans and runs her hands up his body from his hips up his sides to his neck, where she tugs on him, pulling him down toward her.

He gives in and follows her lead, arching his back so he doesn't put his weight on her, and she kisses him, slow and sweet. He can't help the moan that escapes his own lips as he feels her tighten and respond to the pleasure he's providing her.

"I want to see you," he says as he pulls back from her kiss.

Her eyelids are heavy, but she opens them to meet his eyes, vibrant and blue. Pleasure and desire pass between them at the same time she feels herself building, climbing toward something beyond anything she's ever felt before. The intensity is too much and she moans again, her eyes rolling up and closing just as her sex clamps down hard.

He picks up his pace, moving inside of her faster and faster with each short breath they take. Sweat covers both of their bodies.

She opens her eyes again to see him: His eyes are closed, immense pleasure on his face. His hair is a mess and falling down over his forehead.

Just as she reaches up to brush his hair away, he opens his eyes, and that emotion, the one she couldn't identify before, is there again, only this time she knows it for what it is. She can feel the same emotion building up inside of her. Love and adoration.

With each thrust of his hips, Vivienne's pleasure builds and builds, climbing higher and higher. Then, just like that, the pleasure peaks. Her eyes close and she moans louder, arching her back to the pleasure she feels deep inside.

In a second they both come unraveled, lost in the climax, and Mikah pours himself into her.

FOURTEEN

They are both breathing heavily, and neither one says anything for some time. Staring deep into each other's eyes, they know nothing needs to be said. It's there, between them, everything they've been fighting emotionally since they met.

Vivienne's never experienced anything like this before, has never known what real, raw desire and love truly feel like. Somewhere along their journey, she's fought it, fought to embrace it, to accept the fact that she could be deserving of more, but he makes it clearer to her now; it's in his eyes.

Destiny. That's what this feels like to Mikah. And the look in her eyes now is all he needs. He will do anything for her, anything to protect her, no matter what the cost.

Once their breathing finally returns to normal, Mikah slowly slides out of Vivienne. She winces and shivers at the loss.

"Did I hurt you?" he whispers.

"No," she says back to him as he rolls to her side.

He snakes his arm in under her head and she snuggles into him. He pulls the covers up to cover them and brings one hand to rest on her belly.

She smiles.

"Are you feeling okay?"

She blushes. "I feel great," she says and kisses his chest. She puts her hand over his.

He smiles at her. "Good." He kisses the top of her forehead and settles in with her. He knows now what all of this emotion has been building toward.

That first night, in the diner, he found a woman who wasn't helpless but who maybe needed a little bit of help to get through. There was something special about her; he felt it in places that he'd long since forgotten. When his mother died, he built up walls of determination that made loving another woman nearly impossible. He'd tried, but there'd been nothing like what he feels right now.

He'd gone back the next night with no prompting from his wings. He'd just wanted to see her again. He kept going back because the wanting became needing. He knew it then – that she was something special - and now...now she's here, in his arms and in his bed. He meant what he said: He will stop at nothing to protect her, to make her safe, and no matter what, he will always be here for her, for both of them.

Vivienne tilts her head toward him. His eyes are closed, but his hand rubs lightly along her belly, sending goose bumps across her skin and a warmth into her heart. Her life has changed so much in such a short time; she can't imagine going through all of this with anyone but him. To have him here to help her, to protect her and to guide her is exactly what she needed.

She pulls her hand away from Mikah's and begins to trace the lines of his chest. Doing so reminds her of his chest in their dreams, the tattoo that runs over his right shoulder. She wonders where it comes from.

She hears his breathing hitch a little with some of her strokes, but she doesn't stop, and when she looks up at him he's smiling.

He begins to do the same, trailing his fingers along her belly, down over her hips, across her pelvic bone and up the other side. His fingers are light against her skin, and her nipples harden.

He continues tracing the lines of her body, carefully avoiding all of those spots that would send her over the edge. Her caresses have stirred his erection once again, but he's not sure how she'd feel about a round two. He's content to touch her in any way he can.

She writhes beneath the slow, sensual patterns he is making along her skin, which has been made even more sensitive by the explosive orgasm she experienced not all that long ago. The desire she feels for him is building once again, and she can feel his erection pressed against her thigh between them, but since he hasn't made a move to intensify the contact between them, she's not entirely sure what to make of it.

She can't see his body and he can't see hers, but their touching continues until the pleasure closes their eyes one last time and they fall asleep in each other's arms.

FIFTEEN

.

Around noon, Vivienne begins to stir in Mikah's arms. One of his legs is draped over her, and his arms are both wrapped around her. She takes a deep breath, breathing in his scent: sweet and heady and simply Mikah.

She fights the urge to squirm. She really needs to go to the bathroom, but he's sleeping so peacefully – something she's never seen before because he always manages to wake up before her - that the idea of waking him nearly breaks her heart. He looks so innocent. The beautifully tanned skin of his bare chest begs her to touch it.

Last night feels like a dream and miles away from right now. She'd come home from the spa trip with Celeste to find her apartment lined with candles, the pictures, the bracelet, and then the clothes, that dress, the one she always seems to be wearing in Elysium. Then taking her to the charity gala. Did she really tell him that she'd go back to school and eventually work for him? She smiles at the memory of the evening and where it had been going...at least until Red had interrupted them.

Going to Elysium and having Mikah find out about nearly everything makes her a little anxious. She knows that she still needs to tell him about the shifter.

She also knows that at some point she wants to speak with Elizabeth about talking to her mother in private. This, Vivienne knows, will not be an easy thing, but it is important. Vivienne would never have gotten to talk with her mother while she was still alive, at least not with any real conversation or comprehension. Maybe this is her chance to tell her mother how she feels, at the very least.

Her bladder finally overcomes her desire to let Mikah sleep, and Vivienne squirms involuntarily.

Mikah stirs. His blue eyes meet hers and a smile spreads across his lips. Vivienne swallows the thoughts of her mother and smiles back at him.

"Good morning, beautiful." he whispers, his voice groggy from sleep.

She smiles wider at his vulnerability. "Good morning," she says back.

"How'd you sleep?" he says as he slowly peels himself off of her.

There is both joy at being free so she can use the bathroom and sadness at the loss of their connection.

"What's wrong?" he asks.

She blushes. "I have to use the bathroom."

"Oh," he says, and he pulls back to free her completely. "Sorry." He smiles sheepishly.

She runs her finger along the bridge of his nose. "Don't be." She climbs out of bed and heads for the bathroom.

Weeks ago, when Vivienne crawled onto Mikah's cot in the hospital room that night, he savored it, afraid it was a momentary weakness on her part and that it would never happen again. But this morning outshines anything he felt that night.

Her bright blue eyes, messy, bright red hair and beautiful smile stop his heart. He'd tried so hard to control himself, to not rush through being with her the first time, but being with her was exquisite in the most delicious way he could've ever imagined. After last night he was worried about how she'd feel toward him this morning, but she is here with him.

The morning-after bliss clouds his memory of the other events of last evening. So much happened in Elysium, but it will be dealt with tomorrow. Today he wants to spend with Vivienne, whether in bed all day or out of it. Today is their day.

He rubs his eyes, getting rid of the crusty sleep, and stretches. He looks over at the nightstand. The clock says 12:33p.m. He smiles. It has been probably ten years since he's slept until after noon.

Vivienne steps into his field of vision and he smiles at her. Her answering smile is warm.

"How are you feeling?" he asks.

"Good. Still tired, but I feel great."

"You look amazing," he says, his hungry eyes roam over her naked form standing at the foot of the bed. He laughs a little when she realizes that she's naked.

"Jeez, thanks for reminding me." She scurries into the bed and under the covers.

"Never cover yourself for me. I think you're beautiful." He kisses her on the forehead and pulls the covers back. "My turn."

He quickly jumps out of bed, giving her a view of his beautiful, well-sculpted ass as he disappears into the bathroom. She blushes and buries herself under the covers.

Mikah emerges from the bathroom and leans on the doorjamb, watching to see if she'll emerge from her hiding place under the covers. When she doesn't stir, he decides to play with her. He creeps to the foot of the bed. When he lifts up the comforter, she giggles. The sheet is still between them, but looking up her body, he can see the swell of her belly. It's one of the most beautiful things he's ever seen.

He climbs onto the bed under the comforter and snakes his way up her body, kissing and breathing hotly through the sheet between them, and she giggles again. When he reaches her belly he kisses it, then reaches up to pull the sheet back. She helps him lower it.

Still underneath the comforter, she stares down into his beautiful blue eyes. He looks so sweet and boyish hiding under the covers, his hair all mussed up. The image is breathtaking, and the now-familiar ache from last night returns.

Mikah senses her shift in mood. He slides up a little further until his mouth is even with hers. His kiss is filled with passionate promises of what's to come.

SIXTEEN

Sometime later they emerge from under the comforter, sweaty and breathing heavily. Neither one of them speaks until their heart rates calm down and their breathing returns to normal.

"Are you hungry?"

Vivienne laughs a little bit. "I'm starving," she says, and he smiles back at her.

"We can't have that. How about breakfast in bed?"

She laughs a little harder. "Breakfast? Mikah, it's nearly two in the afternoon."

He laughs with her. "You're right, but it's never too late for breakfast."

He flings the covers aside, sits on the edge of the bed and looks around for his pants. "Hmm," he says when he can't find them. He gives up, deciding instead to give Vivienne another show. He stands and walks toward the closet. When she realizes that he's walking around naked, she hides under the covers again, giggling.

Mikah grabs two pairs of pants, one for him and one for her. He also grabs one of his Boston College t-shirts for her to throw on.

"Here you go, sweetheart," he says, emerging from the closet. "I'll have Celeste and the boys bring your stuff up from the condo downstairs, but in the meantime, here's a pair of my pants and a t-shirt for you."

She peeks coquettishly out from under the covers and giggles again.

He laughs. "You silly girl."

She smiles and he leans down to kiss her. She kisses him back, remembering all too clearly the last hour or so spent under the sheets.

But he doesn't linger.

"Mind if I take a shower?" she asks.

"Never ask me, my home is your home. Please, make yourself comfortable. I'll be back in a bit with food," he says as he reaches the door.

As soon as he leaves the room Vivienne is desperate to see him again, but instead she climbs out of bed and takes the clothes Mikah's laid out for her into the bathroom.

Mikah isn't in the kitchen very long when he hears the running water of the shower. Smiling at the idea of Vivienne in his shower, he opens the fridge. He's moving a few things around when Celeste comes around the corner.

"Can I help you, Mikah?"

He jumps at her voice and grazes his head on the door of the fridge in his haste to stand and turn around.

"Good morning, Celeste."

"Afternoon, sir," she says with a grin.

He laughs. "No, I think I can handle some bacon, eggs and toast."

"Of course." She hesitates a moment. "Mikah, I just wanted to apologize. For last night."

He cocks his head at her.

"Neither Red nor I nor any of us had any intention of having to spring who and what we are on you like that. We wanted to wait until you were comfortable with being an angel before we sat down to discuss it with you."

"Stop. Though I don't appreciate being kept of out things and I'm not certain I've grasped all of this angel stuff yet, I'm not angry. But I am curious as to how Vivienne found out before I did."

Celeste looks uncomfortable for a moment. "I suggest you ask Vivienne about that. It's not my place to explain it."

"Fair enough."

"Do you need anything else?" she asks, changing the subject.

"Can you and the boys clean out the apartment downstairs? Bring up whatever you need from down there, plus all of Vivienne's things?" he asks, his voice gentler than when they first started talking.

"It's already been done. Her stuff is in the second bedroom. I will move it over to your room, if you'd like, when you're not in the bedroom."

"Please?"

She nods.

"Thank you, Celeste."

"Anything, anytime. Anything else?"

"No, I'm good. I think we're going to spend the day in bed or in the TV room."

"Sounds good."

The shower turns off and Celeste takes that as a cue to leave. She heads down the hall toward the door, and Mikah goes about starting their breakfast.

Vivienne towels off and gets dressed. Her hair is still soaking wet, so she wraps it up in her towel and piles it on top of her head. She smells like Mikah – well, at least his body wash – and she savors the scent.

The last twenty-four hours have been a whirlwind of events, and when she woke up yesterday, she never imagined that this morning she would wake up with Mikah. She smiles into the mirror as she throws on Mikah's Boston College t-shirt and turns to leave the bathroom, knowing that Mikah is probably waiting for her in bed.

When she steps out of the bathroom, though, he isn't there. She can smell bacon frying, so she heads for the kitchen.

When she opens the door she hears shifting and plates being set down, followed by the popping sound of the toaster. She comes around the corner of the kitchen to see him standing over the stove stirring something. She smiles because he's still shirtless and his wings are shimmering in the light over the center bar.

"Smells wonderful," she says, and Mikah jumps just a little bit. She giggles. "I didn't mean to scare you."

He turns toward her, taking in the beautiful sight of her in his t-shirt, her hair up in a towel, and the beautiful smile on her face. "Feeling better?"

She nods. "The shower felt great, thank you."

He comes around the counter and wraps his arms around her. "I said we'd have breakfast in bed." He kisses the top of her forehead. "So why don't you go lie back down, get comfortable, and I will be in in just a couple of minutes."

"But I like watching you cook," she grumbles against his chest.

He laughs. "There's plenty of time to watch me cook. Go on. I want to serve you breakfast in bed."

"Hmph," she huffs.

She stalks off toward the bedroom and he laughs at his fiery tiger.

Guessing the direction of his thoughts, she can't help but smile to herself as she crosses the threshold into the bedroom.

SEVENTEEN

"What would you like to do today?" he asks as he wipes his mouth and hands with a napkin. He places the napkin back on the tray he's brought into the bedroom, and then his hand seeks hers.

"Do you have work to do?"

He scowls at her question. "Today is just for us. I'd had plans to take you shopping today, get some more clothes for you, but I think it would be better if we stayed in the condo."

She thinks about this and finds that she's not at all upset about the idea of him buying her more clothes. Everything's different between them since last night, and suddenly it feels okay. Though perhaps part of the reason it feels okay is because they won't actually be going shopping.

"I'd like to get my stuff from the condo downstairs," she says.

"Already done. Celeste had it all brought up and placed in the second bedroom while we were sleeping." He winks at her and she blushes. "I'd like to have her move your clothes over here into my closet, if you'd like that?" The question is already out before he can stop himself, and only then does he begin to feel uneasy. He didn't mean to ask her to make a decision about whether to stay with him and live out of the same bedroom so soon.

His question surprises her, but she can see in his face that he is a little concerned about her response, so she smiles at him. "Is there room in there?" She points toward the closet.

He laughs. "No, but they can make room. There are a lot of clothes in there that I no longer wear. I'll have them removed and donated, and you can have space in there too."

She likes the idea of him making room for her and is pleased that it doesn't seem to come at a personal cost or inconvenience, such as having to go into the second bedroom for his own clothes. "Alright," she says.

He leans over and kisses her, this time square on the lips. "Now that's resolved. But we still haven't answered the question about what we'll do today."

She smiles and shakes her head. "Did you have something in mind?"

He wiggles his eyebrows at her and she blushes.

Then he says, "Want to watch some movies? Play around with your new laptop?"

Vivienne had forgotten about the super expensive laptop until Mikah mentioned it and it's not something she wants to mess with today, maybe tomorrow. She thinks for a moment, then says, "How about we watch a movie, then see what we feel up to after that?"

There isn't a TV in the bedroom, which will make what Mr. Wiggly Eyebrows Suggestive Glances hinted at more difficult. Though, now she thinks of it, she's not sure she doesn't want him to succeed, either.

"You got it, sweetheart. Let me take the tray into the kitchen. Do you remember where the TV room is?"

She thinks hard for a minute, trying to remember from the first time she was here. "Down the hallway on the left?" she says.

He smiles and nods at her. "Why don't you go in there and get comfortable. I will put this stuff in the kitchen and be there in a few minutes."

"Okay," she says, and they crawl out of bed together.

EIGHTEEN

Just as the closing credits begin to run on their movie, Mikah's wings buzz in a warm, familiar fashion. It's the same sensation he's felt when Red makes an appearance, but something about him charging into the house warns him that something's happened.

Vivienne notices Mikah's change in demeanor and she too senses Red coming into the house.

Both of them relax until Mikah takes in the look on Red's face.

"We have a bit of an issue," Red says quickly. "I didn't want to bother you today, but can you turn the TV to channel eleven?"

"Uh, sure," Mikah says as he sits up. He takes up the remote and presses a button to change the channel.

The TV flickers with images of a building. Remnants of a fire, it looks like, smoke still billowing off of the roof. "We are live at the home of Elton Bennett, a prominent local businessman in Minneapolis. Police received a call from the home's security system and responded to find the house going up in flames. Despite the internal sprinkler system, the home appears to be a complete loss.

"Police are currently looking into the situation. However, fire crews found what appear to be human remains inside of the home. Now, it is unclear whose remains they are, but Mr. Bennett's security team says that Mr. Bennett was home alone at the time of the fire. All security footage from within the home has been turned over to Minneapolis Police, and they are asking anyone with information to come forward.

"They are also on the lookout for Elton Bennett's son, Riley Bennett, who is wanted for questioning in a triple homicide and attempted murder case from about a month ago. Police are asking for any information on his whereabouts—"

Mikah hits the power button on the TV "Why would he kill his own father?" he asks out loud.

"I'd wager a guess that his father probably pissed him off. More than likely he went to his father to seek refuge, but with everything Elton's suffered as a result of Riley's choices, I'd like to think that Elton wasn't very welcoming."

"I'd hope not, but we all know how they work. Elton has defended his son for years, protecting him, finding him the best attorney. Why would he stop now?" Mikah counters.

Vivienne is silent, not entirely understanding the situation but feeling vaguely and irrationally guilty. Yet another life lost at the hands of Riley.

"Elton's never lost so much as he has in the last month," Red says in response to Mikah's question. "With his son labeled a cop killer and wanted for murder of three people and the attempted murder of another, Elton's political career is over. No amount of damage control can right that ship. Couple all of that with you backing out of the condo project that was set to make him millions and give him the financial power he needed to proceed with his political ambitions, and I'd imagine that he'd be pretty pissed."

Mikah can feel a shift in Vivienne – not just physically, but emotionally too – and he remembers he hasn't told her about his confrontation with Elton at the hospital, nor about all the behind-the-scenes things that MSB has done to destroy Elton's career. But her mood is not one of anger, as he'd expected, but awe.

"You—" The words are difficult for her to get out. "When did you pull out of Elton's condo project?" she asks, her voice weak. She needs to know if it was in retaliation for what Riley did to her.

"The night you were attacked."

Vivienne flinches, remembering.

"The cops came here to the condo," he continues, "questioning me because of the car Red was in when he drove by your home."

"It wasn't you in the car?" she says, a little disappointed.

"All the other nights, yes it was. I was caught up at a dinner function that night, so I sent Red in my place."

A sense of relief washes over her. Knowing that he backed out of his business deal before he knew what had happened to her gives her new insight into Mikah and what he was thinking or feeling before she was attacked. But a sense of guilt still plagues her heart: She was so mean to him, rejecting him, and look at what he did for her.

"When the police left, I immediately went searching for a connection. That was when I discovered that Elton Bennett, who was a business partner, is Riley's father. As soon as I found out, I severed the connection. Pulling all my funding for his condo project caused all the other investors to back out, and Elton lost just about everything he had.

"He retaliated, of course. He showed up at the hospital to confront me. We argued, I punched him, and that was the last I heard from him, other than last night, when he showed up at the gala. But his intentions remain unclear. The office has been dealing with it through the legal channels."

Vivienne doesn't say anything, and Mikah is silent as she lets all that he's just told her soak in.

If it hadn't been Vivienne, Mikah might not have pulled out of his business deal with Elton, but the fact is, it was her, and he never thought twice about it.

Vivienne continues to stay quiet, unsure what to say to him, but she is quickly beginning to understand that she means more to Mikah that she could've ever imagined.

"So what do we do now?" Mikah asks Red after a minute.

"We need to go back into Elysium with what we know. I'm sure they're already aware, but I think that we need to discuss what to do next. It is becoming clear that Riley is behind Rebecca's death, and we need to plan our next move." Red looks to both of them. Mikah and Vivienne's confusion and concern are obvious to him, but he can also see in Mikah's eyes that he understands what needs to be done.

"Andrew picked up on some additional activity regarding search efforts for Vivienne, but before we can go after Riley, you need some training, Mikah."

"Training in what? I already know how to fight."

The statement surprises Vivienne, but she doesn't say anything. She's wrestling with a heavy sense of guilt. All of this is her fault, and she doesn't even know how to stop it.

"You do, and you fight well," Red says. "But those that you'd be going up against will not fight in the traditional ways. Which is where Andrew, Celeste, Connor and myself come into play."

Red looks at Vivienne. "Perhaps it is time to tell him the rest and explain what you know."

NINETEEN

Vivienne's eyes meet Red's. Hers are wary. She is worried Mikah might be upset that she hasn't told him about the shifter yet. But Red gives her an encouraging nod, silently telling her that it's alright.

Vivienne nods and turns to Mikah, who is visibly irritated that once again something has been kept from him.

"Yesterday morning, as I was getting ready to leave with Celeste, the phone in the condo downstairs rang. When I looked at the number it was yours."

"I didn't call yesterday morning."

"I know you didn't, but I didn't know that at the time. When I picked up, no one was there, but when I turned around you were standing in the doorway." Mikah's face scrunches up, puzzled. "Only it wasn't really you. That's when Connor and Andrew appeared. And, within a matter of a few heartbeats, so did Red." Vivienne watches as Mikah looks from her to Red and back again, no doubt wondering how Red could have been on the plane with him and in Vivienne's condo at the same time. "When

Red showed up, he protected me while Andrew and Connor took out the shifter."

"Shifter?" Mikah says.

"In a minute," Red replies.

"Red then pulled me into Elysium, where he explained it all to me. However, I'd already had an idea what they – the guardians – were because Zirah had told me earlier that morning." Vivienne begins fidgeting with her hands. "Red, Andrew, Connor and Celeste all have the ability to protect us in ways I've never imagined. Red was able to camouflage me so that the shifter couldn't actually see me even though I was there."

Mikah looks to Red, confused. "Why am I only finding out about this now?"

The irritation in his voice sends a shiver through Vivienne.

"We wanted the time to be right." Red's voice is stern, but there is an underlying understanding that Mikah picks up on quickly. "You've had such a hard time adjusting to what you are that we felt it best not to inundate you. Vivienne's introduction to what she is took place more subconsciously, and her overall attitude toward it has made it easier for her to understand. You like control, Mikah, and being an angel is something you can't control."

Mikah knows that Red is right. He does like control, and finding it in himself to believe that he is an angel has been one of the hardest things he's ever had to do.

"I accepted being an angel because I felt that, somehow, I always knew. Or maybe my blind hope that there had to be something better for me had me believing that anything is possible." Vivienne's voice is soft and she continues to fidget with her fingers.

Mikah reaches over and takes her hand in his. "Anything *is* possible," he whispers to her. Still holding her hand, he turns back to Red. "Now what?"

"I'll go to Elysium, talk to Elizabeth, discuss it with them, decide what to do next. But now that we know the who, we just need to try and figure out the why and the where."

Mikah nods at Red. Red gives them both a half smile and departs the condo.

As soon as Red is gone, Vivienne sags into Mikah's embrace, deflated and defeated by the turn of events. She knew last night that it was Riley who killed her mother simply because it was something he would do, and it proves that no matter what, he is coming after her. That Mikah or Red, or any of them, might end up in harm's way puts a lot of unwanted, but necessary, weight on her shoulders.

"Mikah, I never meant to keep anything from you," Vivienne says a moment later. His eyes meet hers and she knows that he's not angry with her. "I just wasn't sure how to tell you. Up until last night, neither one of us talked about anything angel-related."

He raises his hand to caress her cheek, and she leans into it. "I didn't know you knew," he says. She gives him a quizzical look. "I didn't know you knew that you are an angel."

She smiles at him. "I guess we both had our secrets."

"I wouldn't put it that way. I think it was more that both of us were waiting for the right time to talk about it." He pulls his hand away from her cheek and rubs it along his thigh, contemplating something. Then he stands up. "Or maybe I wasn't ready to face it." His voice drops, becoming heavy with emotion. He runs his hand through his inky black hair. Vivienne watches him intently, trying to decipher his mood. "I'm pretty sure I still don't understand it," he says, running his hand over his face.

"Mikah," she says looking up at him. He's standing a few feet in front of the couch, looking toward the door Red just left through. "I'm pretty sure that neither one of us had a choice in all of this. Maybe that's why I'm having an easier time, but the bottom line is that we are who we are." She takes a deep breath. "It doesn't mean it has to change who we are. Besides..." She stands up and comes to stand in front of him. He looks down at her and their eyes meet. "I wouldn't change it for anything."

Her arms snake around his waist and she pulls herself close to him, still looking into his eyes.

"I'm scared," he breathes.

"Of what?"

"Anything happening to you." His eyes glass over. "I nearly lost you once, and I will never forget what that felt like. I will do anything and everything I can to never feel that kind of pain again." He thinks but doesn't say that he's pretty sure the pain would be worse today than it was a month ago.

Vivienne squeezes him tighter and he wraps his arms around her. She's at a loss for words, unsure how to comfort him. It's unclear what the future holds for anyone, she just wants to enjoy this moment, right here right now.

TWENTY

Around nine the next morning, Red and Andrew come into the condo, and Mikah knows where they're headed. He half expected Red to come for them last night, but he and Vivienne had been left alone to just be with one another for the evening.

"Elizabeth wishes to see us all," Red says as he comes to stand in the dining room.

Vivienne and Mikah, who had just finished cleaning up from breakfast, stop what they're doing and both nod. The four of them head for the hallway that leads to the condo's foyer and there, at the end of the hallway, is a portal straight into Elysium.

"No smoke and mirrors this time?" Mikah teases Red.

"No, there's no need. Portals can be opened anywhere."

"Huh," Mikah huffs as they all step through, back into Elysium.

Nothing has changed in the white room since Saturday night except that Elizabeth, Zirah, Seraphina, Connor and Celeste are all already in the room.

When they come in Elizabeth gestures toward the couch, indicating that Mikah and Vivienne should take a seat. "Listen, I know a lot has transpired over the last couple of days, however, we now know that a trap was laid out for you by Riley. He killed your mother in an attempt to bring you to the funeral home."

Mikah's heart rate rises quickly, and Vivienne can feel the tension in his embrace. She looks to him, hoping to comfort him.

"Riley went to great lengths not only to kill Rebecca, but also in his attempt at laying a trap for Vivienne. He's yet to discover that Vivienne is with anyone. At least from what we can tell. Riley figured that if Rebecca was dead, Vivienne would run straight to the rehab center and she would go alone, therefore giving him the opportunity to complete his task."

"Which is what exactly?" Mikah asks the question everyone is thinking.

"At this point, from what information we've received, we believe he intended to kidnap her and take her back to the devil."

"So what are we supposed to do about him?" Mikah asks. "Can we call the cops and have—"

The look on Elizabeth's face says it all: The police can't stop Riley.

"*We* need to..." Mikah doesn't finish the sentence. He doesn't have to. His heart beats even faster.

"Yes, this is a matter for the guardians to handle."

Vivienne is overcome with guilt; if it hadn't been for her meeting Riley in the first place, they wouldn't be here today.

Mikah can feel her worry and the pain she is feeling in his wings; they begin to burn.

"Vivienne, do not blame yourself, this is not your fault. You see, your daughter— Have you thought of a name yet?"

Vivienne responds by shaking her head.

Elizabeth half smiles but continues. "Your daughter will have the power to overthrow the devil, and the devil knows that. He is so blind to the truth that he will stop at nothing to ensure his survival."

"What do you mean 'the truth'?" Vivienne asks.

Elizabeth starts to pace again. "The battle between good and evil will never end. It can't end."

Everyone in the room looks to each other, confusion written all over their faces.

"There are two reasons for this," Elizabeth says. "One being that the devil, like *Dia*, can appoint an heir. So even if we overthrew Link, his heir would take over."

"Does Link have an heir?" Mikah asks.

"No, though if he fails to capture Vivienne, he will seek one as quickly as possible."

"Why would capturing me be to his advantage?" Vivienne asks. The question that has been bugging her since Elizabeth first mentioned it.

All eyes are on Vivienne, and it seems to her that the others already know the answer.

Zirah steps forward to answer. "Capturing you means that your daughter, though of the purest angelic blood, would be raised by the devil himself, therefore giving him the weapon he would need to overthrow *Dia*. You see, the path an angel takes is based on how they're raised and the choices they make. If your daughter were to be raised by Link, he would have control over her and she would learn no other way but his."

Everyone is silent for a moment.

Vivienne can't think of anything to say. She knows that no one in this room would ever let that happen, including herself and Mikah, which means that Link will have to find his own heir. She guesses Link wouldn't be the type to settle for second best; he'd want one of his own. He'd just need the right woman to help him along in that scenario.

One name runs through Vivienne's head, a name she hasn't thought about since that dream in the hospital. "Nyssa," she whispers.

TWENTY-ONE

"Whoa, who?" Mikah says.

"When I was in the hospital, right before we left—" She glances at Mikah. "—I had a dream. A dream where I was in a dark cave. I couldn't see anything or anyone, but I heard voices. Riley was there, though based on what I heard, he was either dead or unconscious. And someone, I'm assuming it was the devil, was talking to a girl who said her name was Nyssa."

Mikah recognizes the name but doesn't understand the significance behind Vivienne's realization.

"Do we know who Nyssa is?" Elizabeth asks Vivienne.

"No, I never saw her face, but I know a Nyssa from the diner I used to work at."

Elizabeth stops in her tracks and turns toward Vivienne.

"Do you think they are one and the same?" Elizabeth asks.

"I can't say for certain, and I'm not sure I want to find out. But I'm also not sure when in time this happened. Or will happen. In the dream I was pregnant, further along than I am now, so I'm guessing it hasn't happened yet."

Ideas begin turning in Elizabeth's head, and she turns to Red. "Can we figure out who this person is?"

Red takes a step in Elizabeth's direction. "We will do whatever we can to try and find out. Though I'm not convinced she's significant."

"Good point, but I'd rather try and figure it out before Link does."

Elizabeth goes back to pacing. "As far as Riley is concerned, we're aware that he is not acting alone. Though Link has a lot of confidence in Riley's ability to complete the task he's been sent to do, he doesn't trust Riley enough to send him out on his own. Which is why I believe that Riley is meant to kidnap Vivienne and bring her back to Link. But again, it's speculation."

Vivienne takes a deep breath and places her head in her hands. Exhaustion begins to overwhelm her. "How do I stop him?" she mumbles.

"You, my dear? No, *you* don't stop him. *We* stop him." Red says, and Andrew, Celeste and Connor step forward.

"You cannot do it with the four of you. You will need Mikah too," Elizabeth says, her voice a whisper that resonates throughout the room as if shouted through a megaphone.

Vivienne begins to sob. She understands what the potential consequences of Mikah helping are, and she can't even begin to process the idea. "There has to be another way," Vivienne cries.

Elizabeth kneels down in front of her. "Vivienne, believe me, I wouldn't send him to fight if there was any other way. I don't know what kind of fight this will be, but I can assure you that we have the advantage."

All eyes immediately turn to Elizabeth, and Vivienne raises her head to look at her.

"What do you mean?" Mikah says hesitantly.

Elizabeth smiles slightly. "Well, for one, we've taken away their element of surprise. With the level of protection that is in place around both of you, Riley cannot find you until we're ready for him to do so. That is why he tried to get you to the rehab center."

Mikah stands and takes a few steps away, trying to figure out where his mother is going with all of this.

"Mikah, I suggest you both plan to stay in your apartment, versus the one downstairs, for the foreseeable future. Though both are protected, your penthouse has more layers of protection, along with fewer access points."

"Alright, but please tell me that's not all we have in our arsenal. I don't know if that will be enough." Mikah's pessimism drives a valid point.

Andrew chimes in for the first time. "Do you honestly think that whoever was sent with him will leave Riley alone, unsupervised?"

"No, Andrew, I don't think they will leave him alone, at least not intentionally. And no, the penthouse is not your only weapon, though that may be the wrong word for it." As Elizabeth speaks, Zirah and Seraphina move to stand alongside her.

"Please stop with all the vagueness." Mikah's patience is wearing very thin.

"I cannot tell you how your battle will end because we do not know. I can only give you some strategic help. With any luck, that will be everything you need to survive. Our first advantage is being able to control when and where Riley sees Vivienne. We will know they are coming and we will set them up, luring them into a trap of our own. Vivienne herself is the second advantage."

TWENTY-TWO

"Wait, I don't understand. How am I the second best thing we have to beat these guys?" Vivienne stands and walks toward Elizabeth. "I'm nobody, I haven't got a clue how to fight and wouldn't even consider it."

"Though you will need to be the one to lure Riley out and into the trap, you will not need to fight. Your talent lies elsewhere. Over the course of the last month or so, have you ever wondered how you were able to heal so quickly from your injuries?"

A flood of images runs through Mikah's mind: Vivienne nearly dead in her apartment; her lying in that hospital bed; her body healed, almost as if the attack hadn't happened at all.

Though Vivienne was unconscious through the entire ordeal, she recalls that, other than exhaustion, she felt no pain. She was unable even to determine the level of injury she incurred during Riley's last attack, so much so that she had to ask Dr. Alston whether Riley had raped her.

"Yes, I've thought about it, but what does that have to do with us trapping Riley?"

Zirah joins the conversation. "Everything, Vivienne. It means that no matter what happens during the fight, or whatever happens with Riley, you can save your guardians. Your extraordinary ability to heal doesn't stop with you."

Mikah remembers Seraphina telling him that he helped Vivienne heal. But if she's the one with the healing ability, she didn't really need him, did she?

Yes, she did. She needed your strength, your encouragement, and your need for her in order to pull herself through. Seraphina's voice rings clearly inside Mikah's mind and he understands. *You gave her hope.*

"How?" Vivienne breathes. She hadn't healed herself consciously; how was she supposed to heal anybody else?

"We will teach you," Seraphina says aloud to Vivienne. "Just like we will teach Mikah what he needs to know. Though Andrew and Connor are pretty deadly, so there may not be much he needs to do."

"Do we have that kind of time?" Mikah asks from behind Vivienne.

"You do. As I said, you're fully protected within the apartment, and when you go out the same applies. We can drop the protection anytime and expose you to Riley when you're ready."

"But if we're fully protected, why do we even have to expose ourselves to him at all? Or to anyone for that matter? What is the point of all of this?" Vivienne is rather upset. "Why can't we just leave it alone and forget about it?"

Mikah takes a deep breath. "I think I can answer that one, Vivienne. If we don't fight, you will never be in the clear."

"Mikah is right," Elizabeth says. "Riley is not all you will have to worry about in your lifetime, however he is the one who poses the biggest threat to you now. The devil knows that he's found something in Riley. The anger that, for whatever reason, Riley holds against you is a very powerful tool, and Link will do whatever he can to exploit that. If you, Mikah, and the guardians eliminate Riley, you send a message to the devil that even his best men will be unsuccessful." Elizabeth paces again. "Link is too blind to see that evil will always exist, that it has to. There has to be a balance in the world of good and evil. When Riley fails, he will turn to his next tactic."

"Which is what exactly?" Mikah says flatly.

"An heir." Zirah steps forward. "The devil will seek an heir to his throne so that when your daughter comes of age and if she decides to defeat him, the circle of hell continues with that heir."

"What happens, hypothetically speaking, if my daughter defeats the devil and there is no heir?"

Elizabeth, Zirah, Seraphina and Red all look at each other, but no one seems about to answer.

"I don't recommend ignoring that question," Vivienne says, a warning note in her voice.

Elizabeth looks at her, anger in her eyes, but she softens when she realizes who it is that she's talking to.

"If the devil has no heir when he is defeated, a state of anarchy will break out within the walls of hell. When that happens, hell on earth will be born and the destruction of mankind imminent." All eyes are on Elizabeth, fear and understanding radiating throughout the room. "You see, again, it is about the balance of good versus evil."

No one says anything. Vivienne takes a few steps back to sit back down. "We have no choice." Her voice is weak and quiet.

"Believe me, I wish there was." Elizabeth's voice has taken on a somber tone, and Vivienne places her head in her hands again, deflated and exhausted.

"Is there anything else we need to know?" Vivienne says through her hands.

"No, not right now," Elizabeth says. "You, Mikah, Red, and the other guardians can work on your plan. Mikah, when you're ready, speak to Red and you two can discuss training. Vivienne, you will need to come to Elysium for yours. Zirah and Seraphina will be more than happy to help you. I suggest that you don't wait too long to get started. The sooner we can end this, the sooner it will be over." Elizabeth, sensing his determination to be done with this, approaches Mikah. "But you do not need to do this alone, my son. Those in this room will help you, and you will have Elysium on your side when you go."

Mikah takes his mother by the arm and kisses her cheek. He whispers in her ear so that only she can hear it. "I know. And you know that I will do anything to keep both of them safe."

"Do not be a martyr. Protect them *and* yourself," she whispers back. She knows how much Vivienne and her daughter mean to him, though he may not yet realize it himself.

He kisses her cheek once more, and she goes to Vivienne and kneels in front of her. "I knew from the very first moment I saw you, so many years ago, that you were special."

Vivienne raises her head to look at her. Elizabeth's eyes are soft, warm and a comfort, but they are wary too.

"Your strength, your determination, and most of all your heart are pure. Call on me at any time if you need to talk." Elizabeth kisses Vivienne on the cheek. "Go now and rest."

TWENTY-THREE

"What do we do now?" Mikah asks. He, Vivienne and the guardians are back in his penthouse, standing in the dining room.

"We need to establish some type of daily routine for Vivienne. Like walking along the river or going to a store nearby. And while she's engaged in this activity, we have to drop her protection." Red says.

"No. Absolutely not. She cannot go out unprotected and alone."

"Mikah, she will not be alone. We will all be there with her. But she has to appear alone. We need to be able to draw Riley out, get the attention of Link, who will send Riley in to do whatever it is he wants him to do. But in order to do that, we have to lay the trap, and in order to do that, her presence needs to register with the devil's watchers. They need to know at what time of day they can expect her to show up. Once they've identified her pattern, they will pass the message along. Exposing her one time will not draw out what we're after."

"I don't like the idea of using Vivienne as bait," Mikah says, but his tone is more plaintive now than commanding.

Vivienne looks at Mikah. "We have no other choice."

She's right of course, and Mikah knows it, but fear grips him; he is putting her in danger, something he swore to himself he would never do again.

"She's right, Mikah, we have no other choice," says Red.

"I know, it's just...it's so dangerous. He got to her once and I couldn't live with myself if he gets to her again." He looks to Vivienne, on the verge of tears at the idea of anything happening to her.

"We have a plan in place," Red says, "we just need you two ready and willing to make it happen. No harm will come to Vivienne, we will make sure of that. We will do everything in our power to make sure no harm comes to anyone, but Vivienne's protection is our main concern."

Red's commitment to keeping Vivienne safe makes Mikah feel a little better about the situation, but still he's not convinced.

"You don't think I worry about you?" Vivienne whispers to Mikah, aware that his concern for her safety could drive him to try and stop this from happening. "All of you? It would kill me if anything happened to any of you."

"We know," Red says, compassion in his eyes.

Something occurs to Vivienne. "I'm not sure that I'm understanding all of this," she says. "If the devil likes control, why doesn't he handle things himself?"

"The devil doesn't do his own dirty work because he knows that there is always a chance that someone could defeat him. He uses 'tools' like Riley to keep himself out of harm's way."

"Okay, so where do we come into all of this? How does our defeating Riley change any of that?" Mikah asks. It is the same question that's weighing on Vivienne's mind.

"The devil killed Riley, thus making him a tool at his disposal to do his work. Until the demon Riley is destroyed by something other than the devil, Link can continue to use him as he sees fit. When he is destroyed, Link has no choice but to send him into hell."

Vivienne recalls the stories of Dante and the circles of hell and wonders idly which circle Riley will fall into once he is destroyed.

"We destroy Riley," Red says, "and Riley is no longer a threat to either one of you, and the devil goes about his task of finding an heir."

"I'm willing to do anything if it means that Riley never bothers me again and I know that my daughter is safe," Vivienne says with more confidence in her voice than what she's had since Red knocked on the bedroom door.

"That, my dear, is why you are an angel," Red says.

"When do we start?" Mikah asks.

"Tomorrow morning around nine. We will have Vivienne go for a walk, and we'll drop her shields, putting her on the radar. My guess is that it will take at least three or four days before the watchers report back to Link. They will be certain that this is a daily thing before they report. If there is anyone they don't want to piss off, it's the devil."

Mikah and Vivienne nod as Red, and the guardians turn to leave. Neither one of them says anything for some time as they consider what comes next.

TWENTY-FOUR

The next morning the guardians arrive around 8:30. All three men are wearing black cargo pants and black hooded pullover sweatshirts. But what catches Vivienne's attention the most is what's attached to their legs. Strapped to Red's and Andrew's right thighs, and Connor's left, are black guns.

Mikah notices Vivienne's unease. "Are those necessary?" he asks them.

"They are." Andrew steps forward and hands Mikah a bag. "Inside you will find pants, a sweatshirt and a pair of boots."

Mikah takes the bag from him. It weighs more than what pants, boots and a sweatshirt should weigh, and Mikah knows that there is a holster and gun inside for him. The gun doesn't bother Mikah – he knows how to shoot; it's just been a long time.

"Why don't you go change? We're going to explain some things to Vivienne."

"I'd like to be here for that."

"No need, lad," interjects Red. "We're just going to discuss what she's going to do and how she's going to do it. Go change."

Mikah nods hesitantly, then looks to Vivienne and smiles. He heads into the bedroom just as Andrew starts talking to Viv.

"Okay, we're all going to walk out the front door toward the river. Once you're on the riverside path we will lower your shields."

"Will I be able to notice the difference?"

"Not likely, but you might. Here," he says as he hands her a tiny black sphere that's about the size of a blueberry. "That goes into your ear. You will be able to hear us, and we will be able to hear you if you talk. We will be walking with you, but you won't be able to see us. You may, depending on your skills, be able to sense us with you."

"I'm pretty good at sensing Mikah," she says, thinking about how sometimes she knows he's there even when she can't actually see him.

"That should be enough then. Today we're going to have Celeste walk with you."

Vivienne nods her understanding and looks at Celeste, who smiles back at her.

As if to prove what she said about sensing Mikah, Vivienne turns to Andrew. "He's behind me, isn't he?"

Andrew laughs. "Well done. Yes he is."

Vivienne turns to look. The sight of Mikah in the black pants and sweatshirt send her heart fluttering like crazy. He looks tough yet so normal. Then she notices that he, too, has a gun strapped to his thigh, and her excitement over seeing him turns to anxiety.

"Are those really necessary? Will they even work against anything that might be coming after us?"

"Actually, yes. They're gold-tipped bullets. Though we're not sure how effective they'll be against the likes of Riley, they should be enough to at least slow him down."

Andrew's confidence is comforting to Vivienne and even a little to Mikah.

"Vivienne," Andrew continues, "once you hit the river path we're going to walk north, to your right, for about fifteen minutes and then turn around and come back toward the house."

"That's it?" Mikah asks.

"Yup, that's it."

"What happens if someone shows up?" Vivienne's voice is halting and Mikah can feel the fear that she's feeling.

"Unlikely, but should it happen, you're Celeste's first priority, even if it means transporting you to Elysium. If it is anyone other than Riley, Red can transport Mikah, and Connor and I can handle it. Better to keep the two of you safe."

Vivienne reaches for her jacket, which is hanging on the back of the stool at the breakfast bar, and Mikah notices her hand shaking. He doesn't say anything as he walks up behind her.

She leans into him. "I'm scared."

"Don't be, sweetheart, you'll be safe. You've seen these men in action already. You know what they're capable of."

Mikah's words calm her significantly, and he helps her into her jacket.

"You'll do great," Mikah reassures her, despite his own reservations. He knows that he needs to be strong for her.

She nods as she zips up her jacket, turning toward the line of men. "I'm ready," she says, her voice surprisingly confident given the fear raging through her veins.

Celeste grabs her own coat and goes to stand next to Vivienne.

"Alright, let's go," Red says and leads the way.

Once they reach the lobby Celeste and Vivienne take point. Vivienne takes great comfort in the fact that Mikah is close behind her. It makes it a little easier to walk out the door.

Celeste leads them toward the river. It's only a couple of blocks away, but there is not a whole lot between the condo and the river. The north side of the condo complex is paved walkways and manicured lawns, trees and bushes. Winter has left the trees bare, but the color of the evergreen bushes stands out against the brown grass. It hasn't snowed much yet.

As soon as Vivienne's feet hit the asphalt of the river path she feels the strangest sensation, like a shimmer across her back. Andrew announces in her ear, "Shields are down."

As Vivienne and Celeste walk side by side Vivienne can feel the presence of the guardians and Mikah in her wings. "Are you surrounding us?" Vivienne whispers.

"Yes. Why?"

Each sensation in her back is a little bit different. She immediately knows Mikah's because his is the warmest and softest, more like a caress than the other three spots. "Mikah is to my back and left. Celeste is next to me, obviously. But..."

"Go on, Vivienne," Red says. When he talks, a spot on her back stings and she is quick to determine that his voice, or whatever he is doing, is registering.

"Ah, Red, you're to my front right."

"Well done." Connor's voice is oddly comforting, though her back's response to him is a little sharper.

"Back right?" she says back to him.

"Excellent, Vivienne," Andrew says.

"Front left," she says. "But how can I feel you guys?"

"Can you feel Celeste?" Andrew asks.

"Not the way I feel you guys, but I can sense her, despite the fact that I can see her."

"You can feel us."

"Whoa. That tickles." Her ear is filled with soft chuckles of the four men around her, and suddenly the sensations have all shifted. "You moved."

"We did. You can feel us because you're in tune to us. When we lowered the shields you became more aware of the things around you. If you concentrate hard enough you may be able to feel more than us, but we will worry about that another day."

TWENTY-FIVE

They finish their walk without incident, and then Mikah, Andrew, Red, and Connor all head downstairs to Vivienne's condo to begin Mikah's training. Vivienne isn't sure what they will be doing and she doesn't have time to dwell on it because Celeste opens a portal to Elysium and they both step through.

Standing on the other side of the room are Seraphina and Zirah, both wearing white haltered pantsuits. Next to them, Vivienne feels self-conscious in her yoga pants and t-shirt.

"Hello, Vivienne." Zirah steps forward, then turns to Celeste. "Celeste, you may go."

Celeste doesn't hesitate; she walks back out the door they just came through.

"Are you ready to learn how to protect your guardians?" she asks Vivienne.

"I'm ready, but I haven't a clue what to do."

Seraphina steps forward. "That is why we are here. Fighting, in your condition, is not going to be your strongest skill, so we're going to teach you how to heal and use some basic protection techniques."

"Okay," Vivienne says uncertainly, but she's eager to know what it is that she needs to do – or can do – to protect Mikah.

"Come with us."

Zirah and Seraphina both turn toward a door. Through the windows on either side of it, Vivienne can see green grass and flowers. A garden.

Vivienne follows them out the door and into the vast garden. It is probably one of the most beautiful sights she's ever seen. Stone paths lined with all different types of flowers crisscross the garden, and between the paths is lush green grass that is soft under Vivienne's feet. Two benches surround a brick walkway around a fountain in the center of the garden, and four pathways lead away from the fountain to arches in the bushes and hedges that mark the borders of the garden. Beautiful white flowers peek out from the hedges. Vivienne can't see what lies beyond that.

"In order to show you what you need to do, we first need to teach you what not to do," Seraphina says as she plucks a white rosebud from a nearby bush. She brings the bud to Vivienne. "Hold out your hands."

Vivienne does as she says.

"Now bring them together to make a bowl."

Vivienne brings her hands together pinky to pinky and cups them, then Seraphina places the rose bud gently in her palms.

"Now, I want you to close your eyes and visualize the rose in your hands. Let it become a part of you." Vivienne closes her eyes. The flower is light and soft against her palms.

From somewhere behind Seraphina there is a loud noise like two pieces of wood slamming together. Vivienne starts. A white-hot flash kisses her palms and she drops the rose.

Opening her eyes, she looks at Seraphina, then down. The rose is no longer a rose but a pile of black ash on the ground.

"What happened?"

Zirah says, "You lost your concentration, and instead of healing the rose, you burned it."

"But—" Vivienne is confused. She didn't even know what had happened until after it was already done.

"This was to show you what can happen when you lose focus. Your ability to heal also has a negative side. You cannot have the ability to heal without the ability to destroy. Balance," Zirah says, and Vivienne understands immediately.

"So let's try again," Seraphina says. "Only this time, once you find the rose within yourself, imagine it opening." She holds up another rosebud.

Vivienne braces herself by widening her stance so she feels both more relaxed and more stable. She brings her hands up and cups them, and Seraphina places the rose against her palms once again.

Vivienne closes her eyes, concentrating on the bud in her hands. She finds the rose – she can see it, touch it, smell it within herself. She watches as each of the rose's petals slowly begin to fall open.

In front of her, another loud clap, but this time she is expecting it and she doesn't flinch. She can feel Zirah and Seraphina surrounding her, watching her.

As the final petals unfold, exposing the center, Vivienne is awed by its simple beauty. She opens her eyes to see the rose, open and beautiful, no longer resting against her palms; it's suspended above her hands.

She looks up to see her teachers' reactions, and that's when she sees her. In the distance, across the garden on the other side of the fountain, Rebecca stands in an archway in the hedge. Vivienne's concentration breaks. The rose flashes and turns to ash in her palm.

"What happened that time?"

Vivienne isn't sure which of her teachers asks the question because she is staring too intently at her mother. "I thought she wasn't allowed in Elysium without an invitation," she whispers to the angels standing near her.

"Who?" Zirah responds and follows Vivienne's gaze. "She's not—" Zirah is cut short by the arrival of Elizabeth.

"She's not. I brought her here to further discuss what happened. I'm sorry, Vivienne, she wasn't supposed to be here in the garden."

Vivienne peels her eyes away from Rebecca to look at Elizabeth. "Have you learned anything further?"

"No, not really, other than she seems pretty certain that Riley wasn't alone. But we already knew that."

Vivienne nods. Two cloaked figures appear behind Rebecca, commanding her attention, and she goes with them willingly.

TWENTY-SIX

For the next two weeks, Mikah and Vivienne train during the day, Vivienne in Elysium with Zirah and Seraphina and sometimes Celeste, and Mikah with Andrew, Connor and Red in the condo downstairs, which now looks more like a karate studio than an apartment. The tension builds as each day passes and they continue wait for Riley or one of the devil's other minions to make a move.

Vivienne's bump is no longer just a bump. Now, at twenty-one weeks, she's grown quite the belly, and Mikah spends every moment he can talking to or playing music for the baby. Her kicks get stronger everyday.

In order to ensure that Vivienne and the baby will have everything they need in the event that something happens to Mikah, he talks to Red and Andrew about his wishes. This is not an easy conversation for any of them.

Every morning they take their walk along the river, each day a little longer than the day before. About three or four days into the routine, they add an evening walk.

Every night, and sometimes between training sessions, Mikah and Vivienne make love. Each time it's a little more intense and emotional for both of them. Mikah knows he loves her and is confident that she loves him in return, but he senses her hesitation to say it out loud. He also knows it has nothing to do with him.

Then, finally, she tells him her story about her mother and about Riley. Her confiding in him is the turning point; he knows she's learning to trust him.

One night, with an hour or so to spare before their evening walk, Mikah leaves Vivienne to eat and heads into his office. Only his office is not where he is going. Once he's shut the door behind him, he transports himself to Elysium, something he's been taught how to do over the last two weeks.

He walks through the great room and passes into the sanctuary, where he finds his mother standing at the altar.

"Hello, my son."

"I need to see her."

"Who?" His mother turns to him.

"Rebecca."

"For what purpose?" Her tone is forbidding, but Mikah will not back down.

"I need to talk to her." Mikah had decided a couple of days ago that he needs his own answers so that maybe he can figure out what he can do to help Vivienne.

"Is that really your place, my son?"

"No, I'm sure it's not, but I need to anyway."

"Are you going to marry Vivienne?"

"What? What does this have to do with my request?"

"Everything, my son. Do you plan to marry her?"

"She has to learn to trust and love me before I can propose marriage to her. I'm sure you can understand that."

"I do. But when she finds that she already loves you and trusts you, will you marry her?"

"Yes." Mikah watches a smile spread across his mother's face.

"Good." She gestures toward the door to her right. "Rebecca is outside."

Mikah steps through the door and into the garden. Despite all the white inside of the sanctuary, the garden is green and full of color and life.

Rebecca sits on a bench opposite him, looking right at Mikah as he walks toward her. Her features as he approaches are devoid of emotion.

"Mind if I sit?" he asks her, not really intending to give her a choice.

"No," she says, and she goes back to looking around the garden.

"Why?" It's all he can ask.

"Why what?" Rebecca looks at him, trying to read him.

"Why did you do to Vivienne the things you did?"

Rebecca stands and starts to walk away. Mikah follows, catching her quickly by the arm and turning her around. "She deserves an explanation, Rebecca. You owe her that much."

"It's none of your business." She tries to turn and he stops her again.

"You're wrong about that," he says, emotion raw in his throat. "You see, I care about her. Deeply. But your inability to show her love and affection has her terrified to admit to herself that it's okay to fall in love. She deserves better than that."

"You want to know why? Fine, Mikah, I will tell you why. I loved Red with all of my heart. When I found out I was pregnant with Vivienne, I couldn't wait to tell him. I was dying to tell him. I knew that he would be happy and that we would all be happy together. But I never got that chance. He never came back."

Mikah's grip loosens on her arm. She pulls free but doesn't run away.

"When I finally realized he was never coming back, I was too far along to do anything about it. Being a single mother was the hardest thing I've ever done. I found it much easier to handle her and life with the bottle. I blamed her for Red leaving, I blamed her for my being a single mom, I blamed her for everything."

Mikah's knees weaken and he sits alongside the fountain in the center of the garden.

"I had to live with that choice every day of my existence. I had to live with it inside of my own head at the rehab center, and I had to live with it every time she looked into my eyes. I gave up on her, but she never once gave up on me. Now I have to live with my choices for eternity and beyond. There is nothing I can do to make things right with her." Rebecca takes the bench opposite Mikah.

"I wouldn't be so sure about that."

Rebecca looks up into his eyes.

"You said it yourself, she never gave up on you. Maybe that is still true today. Elysium is not about repenting for your sins, it is about forgiveness and life. Start a new chapter with her."

"I can't," Rebecca says, standing again and turning to walk away.

This time Mikah lets her go.

"She is hopeless, Mikah. She will never change."

Mikah stands and spins around. Vivienne is standing opposite the fountain from him. "Vivienne, I—"

"Shh. She's right. I never did give up on her, but my reasons for hanging onto her were selfish. I wanted her to apologize to me, tell me that she didn't mean it, tell me that it wasn't my fault. I know now that it wasn't my fault and maybe it is no one's fault, but—" Vivienne walks around the fountain toward Mikah. "—but I know that the choices she made were hers and hers alone. I cannot change the past, and I am who I am today because of her. I don't need her apologies to move on with my life." She reaches her hand out for him to take. "Thank you."

"For what?"

"For getting her to say it out loud. Everything she said, I've suspected but never had the courage or the opportunity to get her to say. But now, I know."

"How did you know I was here?" he asks as they head toward the door that leads back to the condo.

She smiles at him. "I'm more attuned to you than to anyone else. I knew the minute you left the condo. I just gave you some lead time."

TWENTY-SEVEN

"You're one lucky son of bitch, you know that, Riley? You're lucky he hasn't sent you to be tortured."

The man in front of Derek groans. Tied up, gagged and bloody.

"Well, any more so than you already have been." His sinister laughter fills the room. "He obviously has something else planned for you."

"Leave us!" A grave and growly voice.

Derek turns toward the voice. Standing behind him is none other than the devil himself, a menacing look in his bright red eyes. Derek leaves the room quickly.

The air in the room warms to feverish temperatures as the devil draws closer to Riley, who is bound to the wall. With a small gesture, the devil cauterizes Riley's wounds one by one, and little by little the bleeding stops. But Riley's grunting, screwed-up face indicates that the pain is excruciating.

"The task I gave you remains unfinished. We know how and where to find her."

Hearing those words gives Riley newfound strength, and he begins to thrash against his bindings.

"Stop that. Why should I let you finish your task? You've done nothing but defy me from the moment you showed up here. Your latest stunt, killing your own father, gives me renewed confidence in your potential, but I don't trust you. If you defy me once more, I will happily watch your balls be ripped off again and again, day in and day out."

Riley squirms.

"Not your idea of a good time, is it?"

Riley shakes his head.

The devil continues closing up Riley wounds. As each wound closes, Riley feels as though a new one is forming.

"She is vulnerable. You will capture her and bring her back to me. If you kill her..." There is a sudden pulling and ripping sensation in Riley's groin and he screams, the sound muffled by the gag in his mouth. "If you harm her in any way..." Again the pain returns and Riley screams, sweat pouring down his face and body. "If you fail in your task..." Riley screams again, this time louder.

The pain is so intense he thinks he is going to black out, but before he does the pain stops.

Riley briefly wonders why his orders have changed and the devil has to have Vivienne alive now, but the fact that his balls are still throbbing with each pump of blood that passes through them reminds him not to question it.

"You will find her walking along the river, near the bridge. Sometimes she is alone and sometimes she walks with another female. You can destroy the other female, but bring Vivienne back to me alive. I will deal with her once she is here. Do you understand me?"

Riley's body is still ringing with pain and he doesn't respond.

"I can't think of any good reason not to destroy you right this second. I do not ask questions twice."

The stabbing pain returns once again. Riley screams out a garbled "Yes!" and nods his head. Immediately the pressure stops. His bonds loosen and he drops to the floor.

"Get yourself together. You're leaving soon."

Suddenly Riley is the only one in the room. He gropes with his hands, making sure that his balls are still intact, and then he removes his blindfold and gag. "One day," he mutters, "you're going to be sorry you did that."

If the devil hears him, he doesn't bother to respond.

TWENTY-EIGHT

Christmas approaches, and to take their minds off Rebecca and Riley and focus on more pleasant thoughts, Mikah tries more than a few times to get Vivienne to go shopping for the baby with him. But she refuses, so in the end he goes on his own.

And boy does Mikah go shopping. He enlists Celeste's help to keep it all a surprise for Vivienne, but it's all he can do to keep the secret himself. He's giddy as a schoolboy.

When Christmas morning arrives, Mikah is up before Vivienne. He brings her breakfast in bed, buying a little more time for everyone so they can get things set up the way he wants them.

Finally, Vivienne finishes eating. The moment has arrived.

"I have something I want to show you," Mikah says as Vivienne crumples her napkin and puts it on the breakfast tray.

She cocks her head at him. "Mikah, we talked about this. No Christmas presents."

He doesn't say anything, just smirks and climbs off of the bed, grabbing the tray before he walks toward the door. "Come on," he says with a smile and a wink.

Vivienne can't help but roll her eyes and smile at him. He's like a kid at a candy store, waiting impatiently for someone to open the door for him. She climbs out of bed to follow him into the dining room.

He opens the door just as she comes up behind him, and what she sees takes her breath away.

Covering every inch of the dining room table is a mountain of things, and it is obvious to her, even from the doorway, that everything on the table is a baby-related item.

She looks from the table to him and back again quickly.

"We agreed nothing for us, but I never said I wouldn't get her anything," Mikah says.

Tears fill her eyes as she takes in the scene before her. There are clothes, bottles, toys, and what looks like bedding. And beyond the table are three large boxes standing in front of a very modest Christmas tree.

As she steps into the dining room to investigate the boxes, Mikah watches her intently, afraid she might get angry with him. He notices how her eyes glass over while she takes it all in. He follows her slowly, placing the tray on the kitchen island as she goes around the dining room table.

The labels on the three boxes reveal them to be a crib, a matching dresser, and what looks like a rocking chair. Vivienne wipes the tears from her eyes.

"There's more."

"More?" she says, turning around to face him, shock on her features. "What more could there be?" she says.

He lets out a chuckle and smiles wide. "Well..." He walks around to her and holds out his hand. "I'll show you."

Vivienne looks at him skeptically, not sure what he's getting at, but she takes his hand and goes with him willingly.

He leads her to the door of the second bedroom and opens it.

"Mikah, it's empty," she says, puzzled. She remembers that there was furniture in this room the last time she saw it, and now there is nothing but bare white walls and tan carpet.

"Exactly. I'd like to turn this into her room. Vivienne, I'd really like it if both you and your daughter would stay here with me." His breath hitches. The way that they've been going these last two weeks, one could assume that her staying here was implied, but Mikah is afraid that once the Riley situation has been handled, she will want to move back downstairs. He doesn't want her to do that. He wants her to stay here.

"Mikah, I..." She turns to look at him. She can see the worry in his eyes. "I'd love to stay here."

He watches as her face lights up. He wants to say it, he wants to tell her, but—

"Thank you," she says into his chest as her arms come tight around him.

He can't help but hold her to him. He plays with her hair, kissing the top of her head. Seeing it all in her eyes, he knows she doesn't need to say it out loud. She only needs to see it, feel it, and understand it for herself.

"Of course. Anything, anytime," he whispers.

TWENTY-NINE

The weather has grown cold and the wind has picked up. Vivienne is huddled inside of Mikah's Boston College sweatshirt and her jacket as she and Celeste walk down toward the river. The closer she gets to the river, the larger the pit in her stomach feels. Everyone seems a little more on edge tonight; their normal walking conversation is absent.

When her feet hit the path, the now-familiar shimmer spreads across her skin and she knows she's exposed. She feels her guardians around her: Mikah and Red behind her, Connor and Andrew in front. Celeste walks beside her, also exposed. With the shields down, she can sense an unfriendly presence nearby, but she doesn't think it's Riley.

After a hundred yards or so, Andrew says in her ear, "Let's pause up here near the dock, but stay on the path."

"Alright," Vivienne answers.

The closer they draw to the dock the more anxious Vivienne grows, her heart beating faster though she doesn't sense danger. Regardless, she's not letting her guard down.

They pause at the dock.

"Are you feeling okay?" Celeste asks.

Vivienne can feel a little of Mikah's anxiety, too, though it's muted because he is protected.

"Yeah, I feel fine, it's just..."

"Just what?" Celeste asks.

"Something doesn't feel right."

"We're all feeling it tonight, Vivienne," Andrew says in her ear. "Let's keep moving."

"Alright."

The air grows colder the longer they walk. Tonight they make it to the bridge – two hundred yards beyond their normal stopping point - before they turn around and start to head back. Vivienne can't quite figure out why Andrew wanted to go on further, but she doesn't question his intentions.

Vivienne slows down.

"What's wrong?" Mikah says in her ear, and she can feel him moving toward her.

"Stop, keep your position. I just want to drag this out a little longer. Slow down a little," Vivienne says back to him. "Something tells me that this is the night. I want to give him his chance to show up."

"Alright, let's—" Andrew stops talking.

The air shifts, and Vivienne senses a force unlike anything she's ever felt before. An evil force. Though it's unfamiliar, there's no doubt in her mind that it's Riley.

"He's here," she whispers.

"Where?" A chorus of voices rings in her ear.

"Ahead of us, along the path. But he's not coming toward us, he's staying put, hiding in the shadows just before the dock."

Mikah's breathing spikes and his wings blaze as Vivienne continues toward Riley's hiding place.

"This is way too easy," Riley whispers to himself as he watches the two women approach.

They're walking casually along the river, talking and seeming to have a good time, though neither one of them is smiling or laughing.

He runs through the possibilities in his mind. Killing Vivienne's companion would be exciting. Killing her slowly in front of Vivienne would be even more exciting. But he's not sure he can kill the woman and still capture Vivienne. Ah, but it would be fun to make Vivienne watch her friend die in front of her. Watch her squirm just a little bit, since he can't touch her; the pain in his crotch is a constant reminder of that.

Vivienne's training had all taken place in Elysium, and when she asked Zirah about it she told Vivienne that Elysium was the best place to learn about herself and what she was capable of because it is free of distraction and the protections she has on earth. The more Vivienne could understand about her abilities in Elysium, the easier they'd be to use on Earth.

Immediately after beginning her training in Elysium, Vivienne had begun practicing around the condo, and she quickly realized what kind of barrier their protection places on her abilities. But the more she practiced, the easier it became to work through those invisible protections.

"Breathe, you'll do fine," Celeste whispers to Vivienne. "Remember what I taught you."

Vivienne had been surprised when Celeste showed up in Elysium about a week ago. She'd come to show

Vivienne some basic self-defense moves. Moves that came really easily to her, and it left her bereft and wishing she'd learned them sooner.

"It's strongest right here," Vivienne whispers as they pass the point where she believes Riley is hiding. Her eyes flicker in the direction of a deep shadow between several boats that are land-docked about fifty feet away.

As they pass the last boat, Vivienne can feel the men shift positions: Mikah and Red move in front of her, Andrew and Connor behind.

In a flash, arms wrap tightly around her, a knife at her throat. "I knew I'd get my hands on you again. Did you miss me?"

"Not really," Vivienne answers.

THIRTY

Vivienne struggles in Riley's grasp, distracting him so that Celeste can disappear unnoticed. Then Vivienne feels the shimmer of Celeste's shield wrapping around her.

"You're coming with me," he growls into her ear, and she can feel him tugging on her, but he's not going anywhere.

"What the fuck?" Riley groans as he realizes that getting away with her isn't going to be as easy as she'd made it seem. His grip on Vivienne tightens.

With one hand Vivienne continues to struggle against his grip around her chest. Though panic is washing through her, she feels remarkably calm as she reaches into the front pocket of Mikah's sweatshirt, where the gold-plated butterfly knife that Celeste gave her rests against her belly, reminding her that her little girl is what she fights for.

Mikah watches in horror at the scene playing out before him and struggles against Red, who is holding him back.

"She's fine. Let her do this. She needs to do this. And he can't get away with her. We've locked him down."

Vivienne grips the handle of the knife and pulls it free of her sweatshirt. She adjusts her grip and then jams it straight back into Riley's thigh, twisting it. At the same time, her wings burst free, pushing him backwards.

Riley screams as the gold blade burns his flesh.

As soon as she is free, Vivienne turns around to look at him, to watch him writhe on the ground in pain. "Not this time, asshole."

He looks up, and his eyes tell her that he's nowhere near done with her. But then he squints, finally seeing what stands before him.

She's an angel! Link had failed to prepare him for this, but suddenly he understands why the devil wants her alive.

"No!" he grunts as he staggers, struggling to stand up.

Vivienne watches his movements carefully, seeing what he intends to do. She can feel them, all of them, surrounding her, letting her have her moment of revenge.

Then, one by one, her guardians drop their shields and appear. Mikah, Andrew, Connor and Red all stand behind her in a semi-circle. Celeste, however, does not reappear. Just as soon as Vivienne thinks her name, her vision shimmers, and she understands that although Riley can still see her, Celeste is providing protection.

Riley's eyes widen as he takes in the scene before him. Unsure what to make of the four extremely tall figures dressed in black that have suddenly appeared behind Vivienne, he tries to shake himself loose and disappear back into hell. But he can't; something or someone is blocking his exit.

Riley pulls the knife from his leg and tosses it aside, glancing at the wound Vivienne's created.

Vivienne watches Riley's anger build, anger at the fact that she's finally managed to fight back. The bloodlust in his eyes is the same as it has always been, but this time it's backed up by the devil's powers, and suddenly his hands are on fire. Fireballs roll maliciously in his palms.

Neither Vivienne nor the guardians can prevent menacing grins from forming on their own faces, and Riley becomes even angrier that they are laughing at him.

He throws one fireball, then another, straight at them. Vivienne holds her breath and watches each of the fireballs bounce back toward Riley and explode. The first one causes him to flinch, the second one shatters as it hits the shield.

"Now it's my turn," Mikah growls, reaching for the knife tucked into his belt. He unsheathes it quickly and walks toward Riley. Red disappears and takes a protective form around Mikah.

Another fireball forms in Riley's hand. Mikah's eyes focus on it, anticipating, and when Riley throws it, he dodges. The fire bounces off of Mikah's protection and explodes somewhere over the docks.

Mikah lunges forward. Riley scrambles to run away, but Mikah is on him, bringing his arms around Riley in a bear hug. Riley manages to get one arm free. Feeling confident again, he goes for the other. Which is exactly what Mikah wanted him to do. Mikah brings his arms up around Riley's upper arms and interlaces his fingers behind Riley's neck, effectively immobilizing Riley.

Andrew moves toward them, gun in one hand and the other formed into a tight fist. Riley manages to conjure up another fireball, but Mikah's grip on him gives him the worst aim. Andrew laughs as the fireball whizzes past him.

Connor begins advancing on Riley too. Vivienne realizes that both he and Andrew are unprotected. Riley launches several more fireballs, but they dodge them easily. Vivienne flinches as one bounces off of the shield Celeste has created around Vivienne. Connor and Andrew seem in no hurry to take Riley down.

Why are they playing with him? Vivienne wonders.

Andrew's fist connects with Riley's gut. Riley doesn't even flinch at the contact, and his foot comes down hard on Mikah's instep.

"Shit!" Mikah growls.

Vivienne can see the bloodlust growing in Mikah's eyes. "Drop my shield," Vivienne says as she realizes that Celeste has immobilized her.

"No," Mikah growls back.

Andrew has Riley by the throat. "Who's with you?"

"I don't need anyone with me," Riley sneers. He brings his hand to Andrew's chest, and Vivienne sees streams of crackling white lightning coming off of his fingertips.

THIRTY-ONE

"No!" Vivienne screams.

Just as the jolt is about to make contact, Andrew releases Riley and disappears. It bounces off Andrew's screen, hitting Riley square in the chest and sending him flying backwards ten feet.

The distance is just what Riley wanted; he starts to fling fireballs and bolts of lightning toward Mikah, who is still protected by Red, and Connor, who is now protected by Andrew. The lightning bounces off their protection and back at Riley, but he's not giving up.

Mikah and Connor advance quickly on Riley, and then suddenly all four of the men are standing in front of him.

"Having fun?" Connor growls at Riley.

Riley laughs. "Of course I am. You idiots don't stand a chance against me."

Andrew laughs this time. "Really? Looks to me as if you're losing this one. But then again that is what he wanted. He wanted you to be destroyed so he doesn't have to deal with your ridiculous ass anymore."

"What are you talking about?" Riley spats, but Vivienne can see his determination waver.

"We know who and what you are, Riley. When you killed your father you pissed him off, didn't you?" Mikah says.

Riley's eyes dart toward him. "How do you know that?" The lightning stops.

"We know a lot more about you and what the devil's motivations are than you do," Andrew says.

"I don't believe you." Suddenly the lightning starts up again.

Mikah rears back and brings his fist around in a right hook straight to Riley's jaw. The contact is so hard that Riley's face jolts to his right, but then he smugly swings his head back to look at Mikah, bringing his own right hook with him. Mikah dodges the punch and connects with a kidney shot to Riley. This time Riley crumples a little bit.

"You see, Riley, we know that you came here to kidnap her and take her back to Link," Mikah growls.

Riley's eyes widen.

"He wants her so that he can lay claim to her child. Raise Vivienne's daughter in hell as one of his own. But you see, we're not going to let you do that."

All four men move at once, knocking Riley flat onto his back. Riley's head cracks against the pavement, but it doesn't stop him from fighting to get back up.

At the same time that Andrew raises his knife toward Riley, Vivienne is nearly knocked over by a force greater than Riley, and Andrew's knife is knocked out of his hand.

"He's not alone," Vivienne breathes. She senses something else in the area, something coming from the same spot that Riley stands.

Mikah and Andrew look around.

"Not a physical presence."

Andrew and Mikah recognize what she is implying. While Riley was already empowered by Link, the devil is now imbuing Riley with the last of his power.

Riley is on his feet in no time flat.

Everything at this moment starts to move in slow motion. Mikah's wings burst through his sweatshirt while Red disappears completely for a brief moment, and Vivienne watches as he surrounds Mikah.

Andrew and Connor stalk toward Riley; their rage can be felt ten feet away. They move lightning fast, and Vivienne watches as Riley's shirt shreds. Then Riley is fighting back, throwing punches and erratically launching lightning bolts and fireballs that Connor and Andrew dodge. Riley's blood drips from the cuts he's sustained from Connor and Andrew. The blood begins to pool at his feet.

Though time feels suspended, Andrew's and Connor's movements are nearly impossible to track, and Mikah stands back and watches, blade in hand and ready to strike when the time is right.

But three things happen at once. Andrew and Connor come to a halt, one on each side of Riley. They have Riley's arms and legs intertwined with their own, holding him still, preventing any movement from him, and Red comes away from Mikah, morphing back into his human form with his gun pointed straight at Riley.

The blood runs down Riley's body as he stands trapped, unable to move, but he manages somehow to throw a fireball at Red. Red, realizing he doesn't have time to dodge it, begins to morph just as the fireball makes contact. Red is knocked to the ground in his human form. He coughs and staggers back to his feet.

Riley's blood loss is causing him to fall weaker into Andrew's and Connor's arms, and the necessity of having everyone here becomes clear to Mikah. He lunges forward, knife raised and ready to strike Riley in the heart.

At the instant contact is made, right through Riley's heart, there is a flash of bright white, and Vivienne watches in horror as Mikah's wings suck in and he drops to the ground.

"Mikah! NO!"

THIRTY-TWO

"God dammit, Celeste, let me go!" Vivienne screams as she struggles against Celeste's immobilization.

Another flash pops near Andrew, Red and Connor, only this time it's on the ground. A massive puff of smoke rises, and ashes go flying in the breeze.

All trace of evil presence is gone. Riley has been destroyed.

"So help me God, let me go."

Suddenly the bonds holding her back are gone and Vivienne takes off running toward Mikah. "No! No! No!" she screams as she runs.

Andrew, Connor and Red all surround Mikah, and Vivienne has to fight to get through them. Finally she breaks through the wall of men and tumbles onto him.

"No, Mikah, not like this." She places her head on his chest, listening, hoping to hear something. But the rushing of her own heart makes it impossible. She can smell burnt cotton.

She raises her head up to see a hole in his sweatshirt. There is no blood, but she can see scorch marks on his chest. Vivienne takes ahold of either side of the hole and pulls apart the sweatshirt, widening the hole enough for her to see five points, charred black, on his chest.

"No, no, no. Mikah, no, you can't do this. You can't leave me."

"Vivienne. We should get him to Elysium."

"No, not yet," Vivienne argues.

The guardians look at each other, wondering how to get Vivienne to let him go so they can get him to Elizabeth, who is his best chance for survival. Just then, a bright white light rises up between them. Everyone looks down, confused.

Vivienne kneels over Mikah, her hands over his chest, over the scorch marks. The light is coming from her.

They watch and listen as Vivienne recites an ancient healing prayer. All five guardians kneel down, surrounding both of them as Vivienne continues to recite the incantation. The men look to Celeste, who nods and mouths, "She knows what to do."

The longer Vivienne recites the prayer the more labored her breathing becomes. Tears streak down her cheeks, and the light begins to die out. But the marks fade from Mikah's chest and a beautiful, intricate Celtic tattoo begins to spread across his shoulder and down his arm.

But he still isn't breathing, and his heart, when she again lowers her head to his chest to listen, doesn't beat.

"Mikah, no, you can't. Please, Mikah."

Failure washes over her. She couldn't save him.

"I love you," she whispers.

THIRTY-THREE

"I'd be lying if I said I was surprised by you coming back through the death channel."

Once again Riley stands before the devil. This time, though, the room is different. It's hotter, and there are screams – haunting screams that echo off the walls.

"Death channel?" Riley realizes all too clearly that the men on the path were right all along.

His inquiry is met with laughter. "I always knew your arrogance was going to get you into trouble. Yes, the death channel. You're dead. Again. And you're mine. Or rather, you belong to the pits of hell, and I have just the person to torture you for all eternity."

Riley could never have predicted what happens next.

Striding into the room is a woman. She's confident, maybe even a little smug.

"Yes. She will do wonderfully," Links says as the woman comes to a stop in front of Riley.

Her hand slides down his stomach as she struts around him, down past his dick, heading straight for his balls. She wraps her fingers around them and starts to pull.

Riley lets out a blood-curdling scream as he looks into the eyes of Rebecca Black.

JANUARY

FEBRUARY

THIRTY-FOUR

"Madison?" He breathes against her belly.

They're sitting on the white couch in the big white room in Elysium. Mikah is lying across the couch with his ear pressed to Vivienne's belly. She's dreaming of him once again, as she has every night for the last two months.

She laughs and nods.

"I like it. I think it's a good, strong name."

Vivienne runs her hand through his hair as he gently caresses her belly. "Madison Callahan-Blake," she says.

His head comes up off her belly and he stares deep into her eyes, not even trying to hide his surprise. "Why?" is all he can manage to breathe.

"Is it not what you want?" she asks him, returning his gaze.

"I love it, but..."

"But she's not really your daughter."

Vivienne moves to sit up. Mikah lets her, then he lays his head on her thigh. She goes back to playing with his hair.

"No, she's not. But I want her to be, just like I want you to be my wife."

She rolls her eyes at him. This isn't the first time he's brought up the subject of marriage with her. "My opinion on marrying you hasn't changed, at least not until after she's here. Then we can talk about it." She rubs her tummy as Madison moves around.

Mikah notices Vivienne's wince.

He also notices that her image is flickering like a bad channel on the TV, and he knows that she's going to wake up soon.

"I want your name on her birth certificate," Vivienne says, bringing the conversation back to the original subject. "I don't want hers to look like mine."

She flickers again.

"I'd be honored to have my name on her birth certificate."

He sits up and turns so that they're face to face, then leans in to bring his lips to hers.

She kisses him back, but the kiss doesn't last as long as either one of them hoped.

Tears streak down her cheeks as she climbs out of bed and shuffles toward the bathroom. Being eight months pregnant keeps her dreams a lot shorter than they used to be. But it is the same every time: Vivienne wakes up crying, bereft, and the ache of loneliness courses through her veins.

Mikah is gone, stuck in Elysium. She'd fought hard to save him that night, but the damage had been too much for her to handle. Despite Elizabeth's reassurance that there is a chance that Mikah can return home, the longer he stays away and Elizabeth refuses to let Vivienne see him during her waking visits to Elysium, the more hopeless Vivienne starts to feel. Her dreams are the only place she can see Mikah, and when she wakes, she misses him that much more.

She believes in her heart that this is not the way it was supposed to end.

THIRTY-FIVE

"How are you holding up?" Celeste asks as they walk by the river.

Vivienne sighs. "I'm alright, just very ready for her to come out. Beyond ready." She rubs her hand along her extended belly.

Celeste and Vivienne have continued to take their daily walks since that day in December. It's become a ritual of theirs, and they have become very close since that night, what seems like eons ago.

They approach the spot on the blackened pavement where Riley was vanquished back to the devil. Vivienne doesn't look at it very much anymore. However, the mark next to it is another story. That's a mark she touches every day.

Though now it is nearly impossible for her to touch it with her fingers anymore. Bending down has become a thing of the past. She's lucky if her socks actually make it on her feet. She's thankful that the cold Minnesota winter is coming to an end.

"What would you like to do today?" Celeste asks Vivienne.

"Sleep." She laughs. It's a sound that has become more common in the last few weeks, but the ache in her heart is still there.

They continue until they reach the bridge and then turn back, smiling as the runners fly past them without a clue that they're there. Ever since that night, whenever Vivienne wants to take a walk along the river, she goes under complete protection, invisible to everyone outside of the shield.

"Have you decided on her name? Last we talked about it you were tossing around Madison and...what was that other name?"

"MaryAnne."

"That's right. See, all the more reason to name her Madison, I can't remember the other name."

The vision of Mikah stretched out on the couch as they discussed her name last night helps bring a smile to her face. "Madison it is." Although she told Celeste some time ago that she was seeing Mikah in her dreams, she doesn't keep her updated on what they talk about.

"How's your relationship with Red?"

"Strained. We're both trying very hard. I think when he looks at me he sees a lot of wasted years, and he's not sure how to get them back. Couple that with— He has a hard time with it.

"Kelly is great, though. She is so excited about the baby. And Andrew and Connor have finished the baby's room."

"I know what we can do today." Celeste says, a little too excited.

"No. We're not going shopping. I'm so tired of shopping, and you know damn well I don't spend any money. You always just go back and buy anything that I had my eye on." She laughs. "Besides, Aubrey is coming at one."

"Oh, you can skip yoga for one day."

"Nuh uh, nope, won't do it. Not to go shopping with you." She laughs again as they turn onto the walkway that leads home.

THIRTY-SIX

"Red asked me to stop by his condo when we came back," Celeste says as she pushes the elevator call button. "Are you okay to go up on your own?"

"Absolutely. I'm going to lie down for a while." She absently rubs her belly as the elevator door chimes.

"Alright, I'll come wake you when Aubrey arrives."

Vivienne nods, and the elevator door closes. She inserts her keycard into the slot and presses the button for the seventh floor.

Standing alone in the elevator makes it seem like it takes forever. Finally it reaches the seventh floor, and the elevator bell dings and the doors slide open.

Lit candles line the foyer walls.

"What?" She remembers when Mikah laid out candles the day he returned from Phoenix, and her heart rate spikes to a fever pitch.

She races to the door and pushes it open. More candles line the hallway, and the floor is strewn with rose petals leading into the dining room, where she can see that every surface is covered in candles.

She walks as fast as she can manage without slipping on the rose-covered floor. The hallway seems like it's ten miles long.

Finally she comes around the corner to the kitchen. Her eyes follow the line of candles to the opposite side of the kitchen.

"Mikah," she breathes.

But he isn't there. Her knees grow weak.

Her head falls into her hands and she can't stop the tears from pouring down her cheeks. She's so confused. She doesn't understand why anyone except for Mikah would do this.

But he isn't here. She can no longer hold herself up as the pain of realization washes through her body.

He wraps his arms around her and catches her before she hits the floor. The scent of everything Mikah fills her nose.

She pushes at him, pushing him away. "I'm tired of dreaming. It hurts too much."

"You're not dreaming. I'm here, Vivienne, I've come home."

Her head lifts out of her hands, and she looks up into his beautiful, vibrant blue eyes. She touches his arm, his neck, his face, his chest.

"It can't be real. I fell asleep, I'm dreaming. I—" She slumps down again and he catches her once more.

"I told you, I will always catch you. I will always be here for you."

All the strength goes out of her and she crumples into his arms, tears streaming down her cheeks.

Mikah has never seen anything more beautiful than Vivienne with her red hair and bright blue eyes. She truly is an angel, and he's been waiting for this sweet reunion for far too long.

"I'm here and I'm here to stay."

"But...but..."

"Shhh, sweetheart." He touches a stand of her hair. "You saved my life. Our life. I couldn't have born to watch you leave Elysium. To see the pain in your eyes every time you knew you had to leave."

"But you left me here. Alone. Losing hope. Losing faith that they'd let you return to me," she sobs into his chest. "To wake up every morning crying because what we had was gone and I had to face another day alone, without you."

"I can't even begin to put into words how sorry I am that you had to suffer like that."

He takes a deep breath, pulling back, hoping to look into her eyes. She tries to look up at him, but it's too painful. It's too hard to look at him.

"It was selfish. I was selfish. I thought that being in your dreams would be better than you having to walk out of Elysium without me. I'm sorry. I was wrong." He kisses her forehead. "I love you."

She pulls back to look him in the eyes. "I love you," she breathes.

He brings his lips to hers: strong, needy and passionate.

She has missed the taste of him, and part of her is still afraid she's dreaming, that she'll wake up and he'll be gone. Tears continue to slide down her cheeks.

As if he's read her mind, he says, "I'm not going to leave, I'm never going to leave you. Let me prove it to you?"

She nods, weak and helpless in his arms. He reaches under her legs and stands up, bringing her with him.

"I've missed you so much," she says. "I could never wait to get to sleep so that I could see you."

He smiles and kisses her forehead. "I know, but now you'll never want to sleep."

He carries her into the bedroom.

"Let me love you," he says as lays her out on the bed.

The look in his eyes gives her hope that he speaks the truth, that he isn't going to leave her again. She begins to let herself believe.

"Are you comfortable?"

She laughs through her tears. "No. She's practically sitting on my lungs."

He smiles wide and tears form in his eyes.

She slides her feet off of the bed and sits up. She reaches for his hand and tugs him down onto his knees in front of her. "Please, Mikah, don't cry."

He smirks at her. "Me, what about you?"

"You know this is real. I'm only starting to believe it."

He leans forward, sliding his hands under Vivienne's sweatshirt and placing them gently on her belly. His thumb grazes her belly button and she squirms. "That's like a hot button straight to my bladder. Be careful with that," she laughs.

Her laughter is carefree and he loves the sound of it. He rubs his hands along the curve of her stomach, and underneath the surface he feels Madison move. His eyes dart to Vivienne's and she nods.

"That's her. That's Madison."

He leans forward and presses his ear to her belly, not really to listen, just to be closer. To Vivienne and to Madison.

"I'm sorry. I'm sorry I haven't been here. I'm sorry I had to stay in Elysium and that I couldn't tell you when I was going to be able to come home. I couldn't bear it, to see it in your eyes every time you looked at me. To know that I was hurting you nearly killed me everyday. I knew I had to heal fully before I could be what you needed." He lifts his head, and their eyes meet. "I love you so much it hurts."

She takes his head in her hands. "As I love you."

She urges him up, bringing her lips to his.

THIRTY-SEVEN

Mikah's hands roam around her body as his lips meet hers. In an instant their breathing becomes heavy and sweat begins to bead across her skin.

Mikah senses her slight discomfort and reaches for the hem of his Boston College sweatshirt. He couldn't help but notice it the minute she rounded the corner. She'd been wearing it that night, and when he caught her earlier tonight he felt the new stitching on the back where her wings had burst free.

He begins to lift it up over her belly, and she raises her arms. He pulls back from their kiss to pull the shirt off and takes a peek at the white tank top she's wearing. It is stretched thin over her breasts and belly. He smiles. She looks amazing.

"Can I?" he says as he reaches for the hem of her tank top, and she nods.

She is wrapped up in the fact that he's here, really here, and despite her fear, she knows he is here to stay.

He pulls up her tank top and her nipples harden. He reaches around to undo her bra at the same time she goes

144

for the hem of his shirt. He unclasps each hook as she pulls his t-shirt up higher.

She waits patiently for him to finish before tugging, wordlessly hinting to him to lift his arms. He does. She removes his shirt and he immediately starts to kiss down her shoulder, slowly pulling her bra strap down.

He switches to the other side and her head falls back. His touch is so soft and warm. He urges her arms up and pulls her bra away from her body.

Her nipples are hard, dark brown peaks. "Do they hurt?" he asks, his hot breath caressing her skin.

"They're tender, but no, they don't hurt."

He smiles and licks the tight bud.

Her head falls back again and she moans.

His erection strains against the zipper of his jeans, but she is more important in this moment. He sucks her nipple into his mouth and is rewarded with another delicious moan. He continues to kiss, lick and suck his way over to the other nipple, which is equally as big and hard as the first. He can't help his tongue from licking softly against her skin.

Her hand is in his hair, holding him to her, encouraging him to continue what he's doing. She squirms under him and he reaches for the waistband of her pants.

His silent command for her to lift her hips has her eager for so much more from him.

He slides her pants past her hips, down her legs, and leans back to allow room to free her.

"Stand up," she whispers and he looks at her. "I haven't been able to look at you for two months. I need to see you."

The plea in her eyes has him rising to his feet.

She reaches for his belt buckle, undoes it quickly, then reaches for the button and zipper. Once they're open, she places her thumbs in the waistband and slides his jeans down his legs to his knees.

When he realizes that she can't bend over much further, he smiles and helps her by pushing them the rest of the way.

"Slide back," he says, looking at her with a mountain of promise, and she slides back onto the bed. Pulling her legs up, she lies on her back.

"Here," he says and climbs onto the bed, grabbing a couple of pillows. "Give me your hand." He helps her sit up then lays the pillows down behind her and she lies back down on them. "Better?"

She smiles, overcome again by the care he is taking to make sure she's comfortable. "Much."

He crawls between her legs.

She needs him so bad, but he lies down and flicks his tongue across her clit. She moans, squirming under his touch, but he doesn't stop.

She can't see his head, which is disappointing, but she can touch it. She runs her fingers through his hair as he continues to lick and suck her clit, and then writhes beneath him as he slides one finger inside. She begins to grind against his tongue and finger. The feeling pooling deep in her core is a reminder of everything she's missed these last couple of months.

Fireworks start to explode behind her eyes and her heart is pounding as she grinds harder, pushing his head downward and tighter against her sex.

He loves every minute of it as he feels her unraveling around him. Her legs begin to shake and then stiffen, and she moans, harder and louder than she ever has before. With her orgasm comes tears – tears of joy, tears of love.

He kisses his way up her belly, careful to avoid her belly button, to her nipples, and then to her neck, jaw and lips. He arcs his body over hers so that he's not pressing on her at all.

When their mouths meet, she tastes her own arousal on his lips and tongue, and she does what she can to kiss it off of him.

After a few more flicks of his tongue against hers he pulls back to sit on his heels. He urges her to lift her leg and she does, though unsure of what he's doing. He brings it around him so that she rolls onto her side. The pressure on her lungs and back eases immediately.

"Better?"

"Much."

He lies down behind her, kisses her shoulder and reaches down to lift her leg.

"What are you...? Oh."

She can feel his erection lying against her thigh. She reaches down to hold her leg up for him, and he positions the head of his cock against the entrance of her sex. She scoots her butt back toward him, eager to feel him inside her once again.

He senses her desire and gently slides himself inside. His need to be in her takes over and he slides in and right back out, again and again.

She can feel every throbbing inch of him enter and leave her. Her eyes roll back in her head and she relaxes.

Mikah keeps ahold of her hip as he slides himself in and out from behind.

The full feeling is so amazing that Vivienne starts to cry, and although he can't see her face, he somehow knows and he can't stop the tears that form in his own eyes.

Having Vivienne back in his arms means so much to him that he realize he loves her even more.

THIRTY-EIGHT

Mikah and Vivienne stay spooned on the bed for some time after they've finished, he still resting inside her. They let their breathing return to normal and he wraps his arms tight around her, holding her close.

After a while she rolls onto her back, dislodging him from her sex, and he groans at the loss.

She smiles at him and moves the hair from his eyes so she can look into them. Her fingers trace the black lines on his right shoulder, down his arm and across his chest to where the scorch marks were originally.

"I'd often wondered where this came from. I wish I'd known beforehand," he whispers.

"Me too. I'm so happy you're home."

"Me too. Have I missed anything?" He smiles at her. "Well, besides you?"

"No, I managed to keep you pretty well up to date. I do have an appointment with Dr. A tomorrow. It's the third of our weekly check ups until she—" She places her hand on her belly. "—decides it's time to show up."

Mikah's hand covers hers. "I'd like to go with you."

"Please? Those were always the hardest days. I knew that you wanted to be there."

"I did, and in a way I was." His hand moves up to rest against her chest, against her heart.

"Why did you have to stay in Elysium for so long?"

"I had to heal. It was unclear what would happen if I crossed back over if I wasn't completely healed. I didn't want to take the chance. Better to be locked in Elysium than never to come back at all. At least that was the way I saw it. But every day that I was away from you was harder than the day before. By the end, I was driving Seraphina crazy."

"I haven't heard anything from Zirah since before that night."

"You won't. You've learned all you need to know. And Zirah is not the best with secrets. Elizabeth was afraid she'd let it out that I'd be coming home. A part of me was scared, when I crossed the threshold, that I'd be kicked back into Elysium. I didn't want to get your hopes up if I couldn't come back."

Vivienne thinks about that. "If I'd known that you were going to come back and then suddenly you couldn't, I think that would've been worse. I guess I had more hope than I thought that you'd return."

He brushes a strand of hair out of her face.

"I know you were only trying to protect me," she says.

He kisses her forehead. "You give me more credit than I deserve. You were left here to suffer alone, just so that I didn't have to see and feel your heartbreak."

"But didn't you have your own heartbreak to deal with? You had to watch me vanish when I woke up."

His face falls and his eyes glaze with tears.

"It killed me every day."

She reaches up to cup his face, her thumb wiping away a stray tear. "See, we both suffered in our own way. But it's over now. You're home, and in my arms."

She stretches up to kiss him and he meets her halfway. Their kiss is passionate and heartfelt, all the anguish over the last two months pouring into this one kiss.

THIRTY-NINE

"What time is it?" she asks him.

"It's ten minutes to one."

"Crap. Aubrey will be here soon."

Mikah cocks his head at her.

"She's my yoga instructor. At Dr. A's urging, Celeste found a personal trainer for me. She comes three times a week. Ironically, Celeste wanted me to cancel today and go shopping with her. Did they know?"

He shakes his head. "No, no one did. Let me call downstairs, have them tell Aubrey that you've had to cancel. I want to spend today with you."

She smiles at him. "You can't hide in here from everyone all day, you know that, right? Besides, I have a couple of things to show you."

"Sounds great to me. Let's take a shower, then we can get dressed."

She nods her agreement and he sits up.

While Vivienne crawls off the bed he reaches for the bedside phone and calls the front desk. Now that she mentioned the yoga classes, he can see it in her arms.

Though she's gained weight since the last time he saw her in person, it's good weight and he likes it very much.

Vivienne heads toward the bathroom and turns on the shower. After a minute more Mikah joins her.

Celeste returns to the condo to find the foyer and hallway lined with candles. She hears the shower kick on and she can feel that Vivienne is not alone. Remembering when she'd set up the candles for him back in November, she realizes quickly that Mikah has come home. She whips her phone out to call Red.

"Come on, pick up."

"Hi, Celeste," a woman's voice answers.

"Kelly, is Red there?"

"He is, one second."

There is a pause while Kelly gives the phone to Red. "Celeste, you just—"

"He's alive. He's here. In the apartment."

"What? How?"

"I don't know, but get your butt up here quick. Bring the boys, I need your help."

"On my way."

The phone clicks dead and Celeste goes about blowing out all the candles. She wants to clean them up before they come out. Dressed, she hopes silently.

Red, Andrew and Connor arrive in no time, having taken the stairs.

"Help me clean these up. They're in the shower."

"Have you seen him?"

She shakes her head as she continues blowing out candles.

"How do you know it's him?" Connor says.

"You know, you can stop being a pessimist now. What is your deal anyway? You're always so grumpy. You didn't used to be like this."

"Lay off of him, Celeste," Red steps in.

"I just don't understand it. You scare Vivienne sometimes and I don't like it."

"I don't try to scare her intentionally. I just don't like to get attached. Sometimes keeping my distance is the best way to avoid that." That's the easiest explanation he can come up with; the rest of that story is a lot harder to tell and not worth the effort. Suffice it to say, he could relate more to Vivienne these last two months than anyone else could.

"That's a load of bullshit, Connor, and you know it. You ran up here just as fast as these two knuckleheads when I called Red," Celeste bites back. "Now, help me." She smiles at the three men just standing there.

About five minutes later they hear the water shut off in the shower and they scramble to finish picking up the candles.

When Celeste bends over to pick up the last of the candles, Andrew is quick to notice. This isn't the first time he's looked at her over the last couple of months. Before, he was too occupied with the task of protecting Mikah and Vivienne, but there've been no sightings of Riley or any of Link's other minions since the night of the battle, and since things seem to have settled down, all the worry has settled too, allowing for other emotions to bloom and blossom.

After the battle, Celeste had become so emotionally closed off that her longtime boyfriend had broken up with her. It hadn't helped that she couldn't explain anything to him. She thought she would be destroyed by it, but in the end it had been the best thing for her.

"Now what?" Andrew whispers.

Celeste looks at him. He's practically bouncing in his skin. She stops for a minute, just to look at him. She's never really looked at him before. Such a professional relationship they've had, but something is different about him today. Maybe it's the beard he's grown over the last month or so. As she moves to put the candles in the hall closet, she smiles at him.

FORTY

"You know they're all in the condo, right?" Vivienne whispers as they get dressed. Right before they'd stepped into the shower, she sense Celeste entering the condo, and while they were in there she felt the other three come in too. "All your candles were a dead giveaway to Celeste. She helped with them the last time, remember?"

He smiles. "I remember, and it's okay. Like you said, I can't hide from them all day, though I want to."

"They've missed you too."

"I missed you more."

"Come on, let's go say hi." She smiles at him as she leads the way to the door.

"Let me get that." Mikah comes around her and reaches for the knob. When he swings it open, standing near the breakfast bar are Celeste, Connor, Andrew and Red.

"The candles gave me away," he teases, and Celeste comes running, bounding into him. Mikah hugs her back, though he refuses to let go of Vivienne's hand, which makes for an awkward hug.

156

"Come now, lass, let the man out of his room." Red smiles, but Mikah can see the tears in his eyes.

Next comes Connor, surprising both Vivienne and Mikah by giving him a hug. "Welcome home." He backs off but then punches Mikah in the shoulder. "You could've given us a warning." He steps aside.

"And ruin the opportunity to get a hug from you?" Mikah laughs.

Andrew comes up to him and hugs him next. "I never gave up hope that we'd see you here again. Welcome home."

"Thanks, Andrew."

"Anytime, sir," Andrew replies.

"No more of that. Mikah is just fine."

Vivienne can't help the smile that spreads across her face at their exchange. Andrew has been like a big brother to her, especially these last few months. She also senses a change in Mikah's demeanor. He's happier than he ever was before. At least when it comes to these four. Maybe fighting Riley together changed the dynamic of their relationship. She smiles again at the idea.

Red comes a little more slowly, and Mikah meets him halfway. Finally releasing Vivienne's hand, he takes Red into a big hug.

"Welcome home, lad. Things haven't been the same since you left."

"I know, but I had no choice."

"I know. I always hoped, but as time went on and your mother got more and more insistent that you couldn't be seen, it became harder."

"I know, Red. I made her do that. I'd have never been able to live with myself if she or I made a promise we weren't sure could be kept."

"I understand. Glad you're home."

"I'm happy to be here. Let's all have dinner tonight." He turns to Celeste. "That okay with you?"

She smiles so wide it spreads to everyone in the room. "Absolutely."

The guardians all leave the condo, giving Mikah and Vivienne a little more time to themselves, with the agreement that Celeste will be back in a couple of hours to start making dinner.

"Sydney will be happy to hear from you," Vivienne says.

"You guys didn't tell her I was gone?"

Vivienne shakes her head. "We all felt that telling her would make it final, and none of us were ready to do that. We all held out a little hope, hope that you would be allowed to return. Red and Andrew have been communicating with her via email, dealing with what few important business matters needed addressing. I'd imagine she'll be excited to have you back in the office again."

They both go into the TV room. The couch is more comfortable.

"Red has been handling the finances," Vivienne continues. "I didn't feel I had the right to do it. Not only that, but I would probably pass out from the amount of money spent each month."

Mikah laughs. "Maybe," he says.

"Except for morning walks with Celeste and sometimes one of the others, I never leave the condo unless she drags me, usually kicking and screaming, to go shopping."

"How are things with Red?"

She takes a deep breath. "Strained, but I imagine that things will get better between us now that you're home.

Kelly is ecstatic over Madison. She'll make an amazing grandparent. Red will too. I think he sees Madison as a chance to redeem himself for what he missed with me, and that's okay. It wasn't fair to him what my mother did, and I don't blame him at all. It's just hard to go from no father, no parent, to now there is one. Same for Red, he has a twenty-two-year-old daughter that he didn't know about."

"So you'll give it time?"

She nods. "I will."

"What about your mother?"

Vivienne shrugs. "I haven't decided yet. Nothing she can do or say will make it right. She won't be able to stay in Elysium, and I can't cross over to see her in heaven, so it seems a little pointless to try and build a relationship now."

"No, you can't, but at some point she might want to apologize to you."

"When that times comes, I'll listen to her. But I came to accept who she was and what she did to me a long time ago. I don't know that I need her apology like I thought I did."

"That's my girl."

"Come on, I'd like to show you something." She gets up awkwardly from the couch and heads toward the door.

He grabs her hand. "I didn't say it enough before, so forgive me if I make up for lost time." He kisses her forehead. "I love you."

"I love you too, Mikah." She touches her other hand to his cheek, enjoying the feel of the light stubble against her palm, and he leans into it. "Never doubt that."

As they walk toward the second bedroom, the one closest to theirs, Vivienne tells him, "Red, at one time, asked if I wanted to move back downstairs, asked me if it would be easier, and I told him no, I wanted to stay here. So one day at the end of January, Celeste dragged me out shopping, and when I came home, this is what I found."

Vivienne turns the knob, pushes the door open and hits the light switch. Two soft lights kick on, and Mikah gets an eyeful of soft pink, purples, and white. Directly in front of them is the sleigh crib he bought her for Christmas. The matching dresser is to his right and a changing table is to the left of the door. Beyond the changing table is the rocking chair Mikah bought her for Christmas.

"We still need a few things for her," Vivienne says. "I've been putting it off, but we're running out of time."

"We are, so after your appointment tomorrow, I'd like to take you shopping."

She wraps her arms around him. "I'd love to."

"Kicking and screaming?"

She laughs. "Kicking and screaming."

FORTY-ONE

Vivienne falls asleep around three, and Mikah sneaks downstairs and knocks on Red's door.

"Hello, Mikah. What can I do for you?" Red says as he swings the door open, inviting Mikah into the condo Red shares with his wife Kelly. Mikah can see Kelly at her desk and he waves to her. Kelly is small-framed like Vivienne, with shorter brown hair and brown eyes. Her age is only apparent in the laugh lines that frame the corners of her eyes.

She stands up and comes over to him.

"Welcome home," she says as she hugs him. "Glad you're back."

"Me too. Thank you, Kelly."

She pulls back from him.

"Everything alright upstairs?" Red asks him.

"It's perfect." He smiles to both of them. "I wanted to thank you for all your help these last few months, and for taking care of Vivienne. I'm not sure what I would have come back to had it not been for you and everyone else. So thank you."

Red puts his hand on Mikah's shoulder and squeezes slightly. "Anytime. I know how much she means to you. It seemed appropriate."

"It was, and I can't thank you enough. However, there is one more thing I need to ask of you."

Red pulls his hand away and ushers Mikah toward the living room. "Come in, sit down," Red says to Mikah.

"I can't stay. I want to be there when Vivienne wakes up."

They take a seat in the living room, Red and Kelly on the smaller of the two couches. Just from the way they look at each other, their love for one another is more obvious to Mikah than it ever was before, now that he looks at Vivienne the same way.

"What can we do for you?" Kelly asks.

Mikah fidgets a little with his hands, much the way Red does when he plays with his wedding band. "I'd like to ask for your blessing to marry Vivienne."

Mikah watches Red as his eyes portray a deep-seated sense of love and protection, something that comes natural to a father. In conjunction with what Vivienne said earlier about Red trying, it is obvious to Mikah that he trying but is lost as to how.

"Mikah, I..." Red pauses. "I'm not sure I'm the one to ask that question. Perhaps you should ask her."

"I plan to, but I'm hoping for your blessing as well."

"Of course, lad. I could never deny you your true love."

"Thank you, Red. Kelly."

"Anytime, anything. I just wish I knew what to do to get closer to her."

Mikah smiles. "It will come in time. Be patient with her. She doesn't know how to handle having someone in

a parental role caring about her. Give her some time."
Mikah smiles again.

"I can do that."

They all stand. Kelly goes back to her desk and Red escorts Mikah to the door.

Mikah turns to him. "Please, bring Kelly to dinner tonight. I'd love to have her join us."

Red smiles and nods. "See you later."

FORTY-TWO

"Dinner was great, Celeste, thank you."

Celeste looks to Mikah, a warm smile on her face. "You're most welcome, it's great having you home."

"Hear, hear," Andrew says as he raises his glass. The others follow his lead. "To new beginnings," Andrew says, and they all drink.

Mikah is overwhelmed by Andrew's candor and it warms his heart. In the two weeks before the night of the battle, the four men had spent a lot of time in close quarters, and as they all sit around tonight, talking about the things that have happened over the last two months, he is reminded of that time. At one point, to Mikah, Celeste, Andrew and Connor were simply a housekeeper and a couple of bodyguards. But that's all changed now.

Vivienne watches Red lean over and kiss Kelly. Despite Red's graying hair, he has a very youthful appearance. Especially when he's with Kelly. She knows that he was being honest when he said he didn't know. If he'd known about Vivienne – or any child of his, for that matter – the efforts he's made now tell her that he wouldn't have stayed away, and she takes comfort in that. But although Red may be her father, she also realizes that maybe a father-daughter relationship is not what they need. Or at least it may not be what she needs.

"How are you feeling?" Mikah whispers to Vivienne as she yawns.

"Great. Stuffed, but great."

"Good." He kisses her temple, and Vivienne watches as Andrew smiles at her before his eyes wander toward Celeste.

That could be rather interesting, Vivienne muses.

"Umph," Vivienne grunts. "Ouch." She's not sure what to make of what's just happened. All eyes are on her.

"What's wrong?" Mikah asks.

Vivienne can't help but smile at the concern in his voice.

"I don't know. It feels like Madison just flipped over and took my intestines with her." She lets out a chuckle. She doesn't want to concern anyone until there really is something to be concerned about.

Mikah leans back and puts his arm across the top of her chair. She can feel his fingers brushing lightly on her shoulder. She looks at him and smiles while the conversation around them continues, and the chatter fades into garbled static as she stares into his eyes. Nothing in the world matters but him, for right now at least.

"Well, I think it's time to call it a night," Red says as he and Kelly stand, effectively ending Mikah and Vivienne's staring contest.

"It's early," Mikah says.

"Yes, but you haven't seen her in two months. You don't need us keeping you apart any longer." He smiles warmly at them both.

Their other friends stand and start to clear their dishes from the table. "Leave the dishes. I'll take care of them." He looks to Vivienne. "In the morning."

They all laugh and place their dishes on the breakfast bar, and they take their leave of the condo.

"That was a lot of fun," Vivienne says as she rises from the table. Mikah comes to stand in front of her, wrapping his arms around her and pulling her toward him.

"That was a lot of fun. We should do that more often," he says into her hair as he kisses the top of her head.

She snakes her arms around him, holding him close. "At least once a week?" she says and he smiles.

"At least."

"The five of us ate a lot of meals together while you were gone, and tonight was the most interactive an animated we've all been for months. It was nice to let our hair down, so to speak." She hugs him tighter.

"Good, it should be like that all the time. Are you ready for bed?"

She nods into his chest. He pulls back. Their eyes meet, and again, nothing in the world matters more than each other.

FORTY-THREE

"Marry me?" he breathes into her ear. They're both sweaty from their roll between the sheets.

Vivienne's breath comes shorter and faster than it did just moments ago when they finished. "Mikah, we've talked about this."

"I know," he says, and she can hear the slight disappointment in his voice. "I just thought that maybe you were brushing me off because I was in your dreams, or that you were uncertain of our future. Do you feel that way?"

She twists toward him, dislodging him from inside of her, and his breath hitches.

"I never felt that way," she says. "I really don't want to have Madison in the middle of our wedding ceremony."

He brushes the hair from her face. "I didn't say we had to get married right away. We can wait, I just want to know that you will be mine forever."

"You need a ring to know that?"

He smiles. "No, sweetheart, I don't. I just enjoy the idea of you wearing my ring, telling everyone that you're taken and reminding you that you're mine."

She smiles at his logic. "Ask me again," she breathes.

"Vivienne Alison Callahan, I promise to care for you, cherish you, and love you for the rest of eternity," he says.

Tears well in her eyes.

"Will you do me the honor of being my wife?"

Seeming to come from out of nowhere, a ring appears between his thumb and forefinger, a beautiful heart-cut diamond ring with two smaller stones on either side. The band is braided. It's beautiful in its simple elegance.

"Yes," she breathes, and the tears spill over.

"Do not cry, sweetheart," he says.

He takes her hand and places the ring on her finger. Once it is in place, he lifts his lips to meet hers, strong and passionate. "Thank you," he says between kisses, and she smiles at his excitement.

His hands begin to roam her body once again, and she is instantly lost in his touch. Desperate to have him inside of her again. To show him that she loves him, unconditionally.

This time, though, he skips the fanfare, eager to slip back inside of her.

FORTY-FOUR

"Okay, three things," Dr. Alston says as she removes the gloves from her hands. "First, her lungs look great, maybe even a little ahead of the predicted due date. Which ultimately means that you could go into labor any day now."

Vivienne's eyes widen fractionally, but then a smile of relief washes over her face.

Mikah feels it too.

"Which leads me to point number two. If at any time you feel pain or tightening in your abdomen, check the clock, see if another one comes. If it does, start timing it. Once they start coming about ten minutes apart, give me a call." She hands Mikah a business card.

"Ten minutes apart?" Vivienne asks.

"Yes. Sometimes you can experience what are called Braxton Hicks, otherwise known as false contractions. Those are usually random. If they fall into a regular pattern, try moving around or taking a shower. If they stop, you're okay. If they continue even though you're moving around, odds are they're real contractions."

Vivienne nods her understanding.

"Don't play down the pain. If you feel something, don't hide it," she says, looking at Vivienne.

"Okay, I will say something," Vivienne says, and Mikah squeezes her hand.

"Lastly, your blood pressure is a little higher than I'd like it to be, but it is still within the normal range. So I'd like you to take it easy. Soak up the chance to lie around in bed, watch TV, read a book or two. Don't do too much," she says, raising her eyebrows at Vivienne.

"I don't do much now. Walking and yoga, sleeping, and that's about it."

"Good, though I'd cut back on the yoga to once a week. Twice a week only if you feel it is helping you to relax. Otherwise, walking is okay, just take it slow."

"No problem," Mikah says.

"You've already started to dilate. Only about a centimeter or so, and that's perfectly okay at this stage. Other than that, we will see you back here next week. Same time?" she says.

"Perfect," Vivienne says as she tries to sit up. Mikah helps her up.

"Okay, I'll let you get dressed and you're free to go. Is there anything else?"

Vivienne shakes her head. "No, I don't think so."

"If you think of anything, just call me."

FORTY-FIVE

"Jeez, Mikah, she has more clothes than I do," says Vivienne, taking stock of their purchases. Mikah had a little more fun shopping than she expected, but it was so much fun to watch him.

"She deserves it. And it's not just clothes." He kisses her as he passes on the way to the dining room table, where all the other bags are. "There's still about six more bags downstairs."

Before he even finishes his sentence, Andrew and Celeste are halfway out the door.

Vivienne rolls her eyes. "You're too much," she says. As Mikah stalks toward her, she giggles.

"But it was so much fun." He smiles at her.

"Yeah, I suppose I didn't kick and scream too much."

Mikah laughs at her. In fact, she hadn't kicked or screamed at all. "You had fun."

She smiles at him. "I did."

Before too long, Andrew and Celeste return with the last of their shopping spree.

"I'll pull all the tags and get everything washed up," Celeste says to Vivienne.

"I'd like to do it. If that's alright with you?"

Celeste smiles at Vivienne and nods. "Of course. But make him lift all the laundry." Celeste points her thumb at Mikah.

Vivienne laughs. "I will, don't worry." She smirks at Mikah, who seems all too eager to dig into what they bought today. Andrew and Celeste take their cue and leave.

Mikah starts to pull things from the bags. "We got clothes in different sizes. Should we separate them by size?"

"That sounds like a plan." She walks over to Mikah and wraps her arms around his midsection from behind. "Thank you."

Mikah turns in her arms to look at her. "Of course. Hey, what's wrong?" He asks in response to a shift in her demeanor; she almost looks sad.

"I'm scared."

"Oh, sweetheart, of what?" he says as he takes a seat in a chair, pulling her toward him. He places his hands on her hips and kisses her belly.

"Of everything. That she won't be healthy, or that she'll come too soon, or that something will go wrong, or that I'll do something wrong." By the time she's done talking her tone is nearly hysterical.

"Oh, sweetheart. You'll do amazing. And anything that could happen, we will deal with when the time comes. But don't stress yourself out over something you have no control over. When she's ready, she'll come." He kisses her belly again and reaches up to brush the back of his knuckles against her cheek. "It's been a long day for you. Why don't you go lie down for a while. I can work on getting this stuff sorted out." He stands, taking her hand. "I'll separate everything and then, when you wake up, we can go through it all."

She nods and he leads her into the bedroom. He turns down the bed and she climbs in.

She reaches over for one of the other pillows and tucks it underneath her belly and between her legs. He smiles, realizing that last night she slept the exact same way, only it was him she wrapped herself around, not a pillow.

He tucks her in and kisses her.

"I love you," she breathes against his lips.

"As I love you."

FORTY-SIX

Vivienne and Mikah spend the next few days dividing their time between laundry, organizing, and putting everything away to get ready for Madison's arrival. Mikah notices that Vivienne has less and less energy each day and is taking longer, more frequent naps.

One afternoon she wakes up and all she can seem to do is organize and reorganize Madison's room, and he realizes that she's started nesting. He watches her work, mainly because she refuses his help and insists on doing it herself. After a few hours of reorganizing, she stops and takes a break to have lunch with Mikah.

"You okay?" He asks her as they sit down to eat her favorite, peanut butter and jelly sandwiches.

"Yeah, why?"

He doesn't want to embarrass her, but he looks down and her gaze follows his.

"Well, crap," she says, and he busts out laughing. "I guess it's time to get the pumping thing going." She smiles.

"I could help with that." The tone in his voice is suggestive.

"Wha—? How would...?" She wrinkles her nose, trying to understand what he's implying. "Isn't that kind of gross?" she says innocently, and his eyes dart away from her. "Mikah!" she says, laughing, and she throws her napkin at him.

"What? They're just so much fun to play with, it just kind of happens when I suck on them."

"Oh, for Pete's sake, why didn't you tell me?"

He laughs harder. "And spoil my fun? Never," he says as he places a potato chip in his mouth.

"How in the world did I not notice that?"

He wiggles his eyebrows at her and she blushes. You're usually otherwise..." He clears his throat. "Occupied."

She has no argument for that.

Mikah watches her as she mulls over what he's just told her. It's rather cute to watch the little furrow appear in her brow when she's thinking about something.

The rest of their lunch is filled with playful teasing. Mikah notes that when he pointed out the fact that she was leaking, she hadn't jumped right up to change. He also notices that she isn't wearing a bra. He finds it very distracting.

As she stands to clear their plates, he stops her. "Leave those and come here," he says as he reaches for her hand, pulling her closer to him. When she's standing next to him he rubs his hand over her belly and breathes hotly across her nipple. She squirms as her nipple cools and peaks.

"You're so bad," she breathes as she feels him tug on the hem of her t-shirt. He lifts it to expose her belly, which he kisses sweetly before continuing to lift her shirt higher. She raises her arms and bends forward so that he can pull it off.

Now she stands before him completely topless. Her breasts are swollen, nearly double the size they were yesterday, and his erection throbs. He leans in, takes one of her nipples into his mouth and sucks hard. She moans, and he is treated to a warm gush of milk across his tongue.

"Okay, I felt that," she says with a Cheshire grin.

He releases her nipple with an audible pop. Then he stands, takes her hand and leads her into the bedroom.

While she's still standing he slides her pants down, and she quickly returns the favor.

"Grab a pillow," he says, and she does. "I'd like to try something. Crawl on the bed." She smirks, already knowing what he wants.

She climbs onto the bed, staying on her knees, and leans forward to hug her pillow. She can feel the bed shift as he climbs on behind her, and then his fingers stroke her clit and then up her sex.

It doesn't take much to get her worked up when it comes to Mikah. She is already ready for him.

Seeing her like this is almost too much.

Vivienne can feel the excitement growing in anticipation of feeling him inside her once again.

He doesn't disappoint her. Before long she can feel the head of his erection testing her entrance. She smiles as he carefully enters her.

The sensation is so much she nearly explodes into orgasm before he's even finished sliding into her. She notices that she is much more sensitive down there than usual. She slides forward and then back onto him, encouraging him to move his hips.

But he doesn't need the encouragement. The second he enters her, he is overtaken by desire and begins to slide slowly in and out of her on his own accord.

FORTY-SEVEN

"Ow."

Mikah's eyes fly open, unsure of what's woken him up, to see that Vivienne is sitting up in bed.

"What's wrong?"

He watches as she slowly exhales and breathes back in through her nose. She doesn't respond to him as she concentrates on breathing.

"Contraction?"

She nods.

He can tell the moment it stops because her whole body just kind of sags.

"I think so," she says. "It's the second one."

"When was the first one?" he asks, a little bit of panic in his voice.

She gives him a half smile. "About fifteen minutes ago. I didn't catch the exact time, it woke me up."

Mikah looks over to the clock. It's two in the morning. It has been a week since his return from Elysium, and today is their next scheduled appointment for Dr. Alston.

"What can I do?" he asks.

She turns to him, brushing his hair from his eyes. "Nothing. Yet. Let's see what happens."

She lies back down, turning toward him and wrapping herself around him, much the way she does with the pillow when she naps alone.

He starts to play with her soft, gorgeous red hair. She wraps her arms around him, and in a matter of moments her breathing settles into a calm rhythm, and he knows she has fallen asleep. He anxiously looks at the clock and watching the time tick by and waiting to see if she wakes up again with the next one. If there is another one.

Two oh five.

Two ten.

Finally two fifteen comes and goes without any sign that she's having another contraction.

He continues to play with her hair, thinking about what's coming in the next couple of weeks. Madison. He's never been more excited about anything in his entire life. Not even his return from Elysium can compare to how he feels about Madison's arrival.

Suddenly Vivienne stirs. She squeezes him a little tighter. He looks at the clock. It's two twenty. She doesn't wake, but he hears her groan and feels her squeeze him tighter still.

Twenty minutes, that's not too bad, he thinks to himself as his eyes begin to close once again.

"Mikah."

He stirs in his sleep.

"Mikah, wake up." It's Vivienne.

His eyes jolt open and he sits up rather quickly, but not before noticing that there is something wet and warm in the bed. He pulls back the covers to find a patch of clear liquid.

"Mikah, I think my water broke."

He rubs his eyes and looks at the clock. It's eight in the morning. "How are your contractions?"

"They're about thirteen minutes or so apart."

"When was the last one?"

"About ten minutes ago. It hurt, and shortly after it, I felt the water. That's when I woke you up."

She stops talking and her face scrunches up.

"Breathe, sweetheart."

He takes her hand and she squeezes it. With his free hand he reaches for his phone on the bedside table. He presses two buttons and the line starts ringing. "Hey, Red. Can you get the car ready? Vivienne's water broke."

"It's nearly ready for her appointment. I'll have Andrew bring it around front. Do you need help up there?"

"No, I think we're alright. We will be down shortly."

"Sounds good. Call me if you need us."

"Will do." Mikah hangs up the phone. "I'm going to call Dr. Alston. How are you?"

"That really hurt."

"You're doing great. Can you get up out of bed?"

"Yeah, once it's over I feel fine, just a little weak." She takes a breath. He can see the worry in her eyes.

"You're doing great."

He calls Dr. Alston's number and she answers on the second ring.

"I had a feeling you'd be calling me this morning. How is she?"

"Her water broke."

"Well, okay then. Where was she when it broke?"

"Sleeping."

"Good, was the fluid clear?"

"Yes."

"Okay, bring her on down and I will get them moving on a room for her. We'll see you in a bit. How far apart are her contractions?"

"About twelve minutes."

"Okay. Don't panic, get dressed, grab her stuff and come to the hospital. See you soon."

"Thanks, doctor." He hangs up the phone.

"Shall I get you some clothes?" he says to Vivienne, and she smiles.

"Unless you want to show me off to the world naked."

He snorts and climbs out of bed. "I'll find you some clothes.

FORTY-EIGHT

"I can see the top of her head, so now, Vivienne, I want you to tuck your chin to your chest and push for about ten seconds. Then lie back, take a couple of deep breaths, and do it again. Okay?"

Vivienne nods.

Mikah's hand is lightly rubbing Vivienne's shoulder in encouragement.

For her part, Vivienne is ready to meet her daughter. She continues pushing. Mikah and Celeste are holding up her legs, but she can't really feel that. After about five more pushes, Vivienne can finally see, in the mirror, the head and hair of her daughter.

"Okay, Vivienne, I want you to push for about ten seconds, relax briefly to take a deep breath, and do it again." Dr. Alston nods in encouragement at Vivienne, who takes a deep breath and pushes.

Mikah helps her by counting softly to ten and then she relaxes, takes a deep breath, and pushes again.

On the third push, Vivienne watches in the mirror as Madison's head comes free of her body.

"Stop pushing," Dr Alston says. She goes to work with a mucus sucker on Madison's nose and mouth, and then looks to Vivienne. "One more big push."

Vivienne takes a deep breath. Amanda places something on Vivienne's chest, and Vivienne pushes as hard as she can manage. As she watches the mirror, just like that, Madison is born.

"Five oh six p.m.," Dr. Alston says as she brings Madison up and lays her on Vivienne's chest. Amanda wipes the baby off and wraps her up.

Vivienne looks to Mikah and he, like her, is crying. He bends down and kisses her forehead.

Then he leans over Madison. "Hello, baby girl," he says and kisses her forehead, too. Vivienne is now holding Madison in her arms, tears pouring down her cheeks.

The beautiful baby girl that she'd been fighting for from the beginning is now finally here.

"Hi, beautiful baby girl," she coos.

Madison yawns, and Vivienne's tears continue to stream down her cheeks. Mikah leans down to give Vivienne an awkward hug and to get into Madison's line of sight.

He places his hand very lightly on Madison's head just as a flash goes of.

"Seriously, Celeste." Mikah laughs and wipes the tears from his eyes.

Celeste laughs.

Amanda comes to stand next to Vivienne, opposite Mikah. "I'm going to take her, weigh and measure her, then clean her up."

Vivienne nods, reluctant to give Madison up, but Amanda smiles at her. She takes Madison with one hand under her neck and the other under her butt. "Hello, little one," she coos as she turns around. She places Madison on a bed under a lamp, off of which Vivienne can feel heat radiating.

Amanda walks around to the other side and pushes a few buttons. "Seven pounds, two ounces," she says.

Vivienne watches as she tugs a little on Madison's leg.

"Nineteen and half inches. You're a big girl," she coos at Madison, and Vivienne and Mikah look at each other, smiles and tears in their eyes.

They both turn back toward Amanda and Madison. Celeste is busy snapping pictures.

Dr. Alston, who has all but been forgotten at the foot of Vivienne's bed, says, "There you go. I had to stitch you up a little bit, but you'll be fine in no time."

Mikah remembers all too well how quickly Vivienne healed the last time she was here and wonders if the same will apply now.

"Thank you," Vivienne says to Dr. Alston.

"It's my pleasure, Vivienne. She's a beautiful baby girl." Dr. Alston brings the foot of the bed back up and covers Vivienne. "Kathleen," she says to the nurse who handed her instruments during the birth, "let's get Vivienne some new sheets and blankets and then have the anesthesiologist come back and remove her epidural." She turns to Vivienne. "Amanda will take things from here, help you get started on breastfeeding and get you settled in. I will come back later this evening to check on you." She winks at Vivienne. "You did an amazing job."

"Thank you, doctor, for everything." Vivienne smiles at her, and she leaves the room.

Mikah and Vivienne both turn back toward Amanda and Madison just in time to see Amanda lift her up and pull the icky blanket out from under her. Madison's back is to them, and they both see it, plain as day. On her back are the most beautiful wings in light and dark purples.

FORTY-NINE

No sooner does the door click closed do they look at each other.

"How is it possible?" Mikah is the first to ask the obvious question.

Suddenly, out of nowhere, Elizabeth appears before them, as if in answer.

"Mom, how?"

"Shh, my son, it's alright."

"Do you know what's on Madison's back?" Mikah asks her and she nods.

"She is special. She is an angel from birth, something we weren't sure of until she was born. Only the purest of angels are born with their wings." Elizabeth says matter-of-factly, and Mikah and Vivienne look to each other, their eyes expressing the same sense of worry. "You needn't be frightened. Though she has the markings, it will be at least a few years before they will start to show, at which time we can put a suppression spell on her to keep them locked down. But we will worry about that later. I just came to see her and to check on all of you."

Though Vivienne's worry isn't eased by Elizabeth's words, given that Madison is still an infant it is not a cause for concern right now. All the people around them are aware of who she is, and the overwhelming level of protection on Vivienne tells her that no harm will ever come to Madison.

Elizabeth comes over to the bed so she can have a clearer look at Madison. "She's beautiful," Elizabeth says, and in an uncharacteristic manner she leans down and kisses Vivienne on the forehead. "Well done, Vivienne."

Elizabeth smiles at Vivienne, then Mikah. And just as fast as she appeared, she's gone.

FIFTY

Two months later.

"Vivienne, you look amazing." Celeste fusses over Vivienne, who is standing in front of a full-length mirror tucked into a room off of the main chapel in Elysium.

Her dress, which consists of a beautiful corset top and a free-flowing skirt, is pure white. Over it she wears a sheer, full-length overcoat trimmed with an intricate gold design that comes together in a clasp just under breasts. The back of her corset hangs a little lower than most, and the overcoat is specially designed to accommodate Vivienne's wings. The dress was a gift from Elizabeth, and as per the information she got from Elizabeth, her wings will be a part of today's ceremony, as is tradition when two angels marry.

"Are you nervous?" Celeste asks.

Vivienne smiles at her. "No, he is who I want to spend my life with, and I know deep down that he is truly my soulmate."

Celeste hugs her gently, not wanting to disrupt her dress. "I'm so happy for you guys," she croons.

"How are things with Andrew?" Vivienne asks.

"Oh, for heaven's sake, let's not talk about me. Today is your day," Celeste says as she straightens Vivienne's overcoat. "Okay, ready when you are. Remember what we practiced, nice and slow."

Vivienne smirks and closes her eyes to concentrate. She can feel her wings pushing out slowly, and she pauses long enough for Celeste to adjust the back of her coat over her wings. When her wings reach their full extension without mishap, Celeste claps excitedly.

"Yay, we did it," Celeste says. "Though getting it off will likely be harder." She laughs.

Vivienne stands in front of the mirror, taking in the whole effect. Her hair, bright red and curly, is pull up in a messy bun. Hooked into her hair is a simple but elegant circlet made of gold with a white pearl in the center. Above the stone, a Celtic knot forms a heart.

Her makeup is subtle, her lips a soft pink.

Around her neck is something that Red gave to her after they came home from the hospital the evening after Madison was born. It is a special locket that holds on one side a picture from the hospital of Vivienne, Mikah and Madison, and on the other side a picture of Madison and Red.

She is, as she likes to be while in Elysium, barefoot, though you can't see her feet below the dress.

"Are you ladies ready?"

Vivienne turns to see Red standing in the doorway, looking extremely handsome in his black tux.

Vivienne smiles at him. "I'm ready, are you?"

He smiles back, and she can see the emotion in his eyes. The same one that was there when she'd asked him to walk her down the isle.

"I am," he says.

Celeste squeals with excitement, and Vivienne turns around. Celeste is wearing a beautiful burgundy halter top dress that comes to her knees. She too is barefoot, only because she insisted on not towering over Vivienne with their height difference. Celeste was the perfect choice for Vivienne's maid of honor. She's seen Vivienne at her best and at her worst, and they've grown very close.

Celeste hands her a beautiful bouquet of three red roses, two larger than the third. Each one represents a member of their family: Mikah, Vivienne and Madison.

"How's Madison?" Vivienne asks.

Red laughs. "Being eaten alive by Kelly, Seraphina and Zirah. She's perfectly fine and happy too."

Vivienne smiles. Since her return from the hospital, she has always had someone to help support her in taking care of Madison, and Red, surprisingly, has been there the most often.

"Okay, I'm ready." Vivienne says as she walks toward Red.

FIFTY-ONE

"Nervous?" Andrew whispers to Mikah.

"Not in the slightest."

Andrew laughs. "You're full of sh— crap."

Mikah snorts. "I'm more excited than nervous."

He looks out over the small gathering of people they've got with them. Andrew is standing with him next to his mother. Well, where his mother is supposed to be. Right now she is loving on Madison in ways Mikah remembers she loved on his younger brothers.

Speaking of his younger brothers, they too are here. Elizabeth insisted that they be allowed to come today, for which Mikah is thankful.

Zirah and Seraphina are here too, both vying for Madison's attention.

Rebecca, on the other hand, refused to come, which was no surprise to Mikah, though he was sorry for Vivienne's sake. Vivienne said that it was alright, though, and she remained adamant that the people who would be here today would be the people who mattered.

Andrew nudges him in the arm. Mikah looks to the back of the sanctuary, and standing in the middle of the entrance is Celeste. From somewhere nearby a beautiful chorus of soft voices begins to sing.

Elizabeth refuses to let go of Madison as she takes her place next to Mikah.

Celeste makes her way down the isle. She looks beautiful in her burgundy dress and bare feet, but Mikah is practically bouncing in anticipation of seeing Vivienne come down the isle.

She doesn't make him wait much longer. As she rounds the corner he sees only a silhouette, backlit by the lights behind her, but it's clear that her wings, like his, are out. She takes a few steps forward and the doors close behind her.

Now he can see her clearly. She is standing there next to Red, and she looks amazing. Mikah can't help the tear that escapes his eye. He smiles at her and she smiles back at him.

Her dress is gorgeous and something he hasn't seen until right now. He watches as Vivienne and Red make their way to the altar.

When they reach it, Red leans in to give her a kiss on the cheek and then places her hand in Mikah's.

As soon as they make contact, nothing else matters, nothing else but them.

They walk a few steps and kneel before the altar.

Elizabeth begins the ceremony in fluent Gaelic. Neither Vivienne nor Mikah can catch everything she is saying, but it doesn't really matter. All that matters is that they're joining their lives together forever.

Elizabeth motions for Vivienne and Mikah to stand. Vivienne hands Celeste her flowers, and Celeste gives her

Mikah's ring. Mikah takes Vivienne's ring from Andrew, and they begin to speak their vows in unison.

"I choose you for life. I promise you my deepest love throughout the pressures of the present and the uncertainties of the future.

You have shown me what love feels like, and for that I thank you. You are everything I need, and at this moment I know all my prayers have been answered and that all my dreams have come true.

I promise to be here forever and always. From this day forward you shall not walk alone. My heart will be your shelter and my arms will be your home. As I have given you my hand to hold, I give you my life to keep."

They slip the rings onto each other's fingers, shutting out the world around them.

"You may kiss your bride," Elizabeth says.

Clapping erupts behind them, and Mikah dips her and she laughs.

"I love you today and forever," he breathes.

"As I love you."

He plants a warm, beautiful kiss on her lips, and thus their life together begins.

an Deireadh
(The End)

EPILOGUE

Two years later.

It will have been two years ago tomorrow that Mikah married the woman of his dreams. Literally. Since then, they've lived in that beautiful honeymoon stage. At least that is what Celeste says all the time. Though she can't complain too loudly, as she too lives in her own wedded bliss.

About six months ago, they relocated to a two-story house in a suburb of Minneapolis. The house is far larger than the condo was, and Red, Kelly, Andrew and Celeste are close by, in their own homes on the same property. Connor moved on about a year ago; his services were needed elsewhere, and he happily took the job and is enjoying his new assignment. About once a month he stops by to see all of them.

Mikah stands in the doorway of Madison's room. She's just over two years old and she is the most beautiful person he's ever laid eyes on. Well, with one exception - his wife will always hold that place in his heart. He watches her for a while from the doorway as she sleeps peacefully – much like she does every night, which is a blessing to both Mikah and Vivienne – and then he quietly walks into her room and leans down to kiss her on the forehead one last time for the night.

Stepping quietly out of Madison's room, he turns toward the room he shares with his wife. Here too he pauses in the doorway to watch her sleep. She is so beautiful.

He goes into the bathroom, brushes his teeth and pulls off his t-shirt. As he watches himself in the mirror he has the strangest sense of déjà vu, but he can't quite place it. He runs cool water over his face, dries off and turns off the light on his way out of the bathroom.

The déjà vu washes over him again as he walks into the room. He seems to remember doing this before, only from a different angle. He shrugs it off and walks around the bed to crawl in behind Vivienne. She stirs a little as he climbs in.

"Hi, baby," she whispers.

"I didn't mean to wake you."

"No, you're okay." She turns her head toward him and kisses him awkwardly.

He runs his hands up her beautiful body. He hears her breath hitch as he touches the underside of her breast, and his thumb grazes her swollen nipple.

"You can wake me up like this anytime," she says.

He pushes the covers down her body, exposing her already hard nipples to the cool air, and she shivers and rolls into him. His hand slides along her swollen belly as she climbs clumsily on top of him, facing his feet.

Somehow, she doesn't know how, he's managed to rid himself of his pajama pants, and she slides her sex along his raging erection. She reaches behind her and places her hands on his chest to steady herself. She lifts up, he quickly and smoothly aligns the head of his cock with her entrance, and she lowers herself onto him.

His hands roam her body, which is swollen and eight months pregnant with their son. Neither one of them could be happier than they are right now.

Lost in complete and total bliss, as he is whenever they are with one another, Mikah has a clear enough mind to realize where the déjà vu comes from. The dream from the hospital all those years ago. Their dream has come true, just like all their other dreams have and will continue to come true.

Sliding herself up and down his erection, she begins to shake as her orgasm begins to overcome her, and Mikah knows that she won't be able to hold herself up anymore when she comes. He gently rolls, bringing her with him so that she is on her side and he is spooning behind her. Grinding his hips against her he feels her tighten around him, and his own climax takes him.

They fall asleep intertwined with one another, like they have for many nights before and will for many more nights to come.

Thank You!

Thank you, from the bottom of my heart, for your amazing and continuing support of my stories. Especially Vivienne and Mikah's.

Acknowledgements

This story wouldn't be in your hands if it wasn't for the amazing support of my wonderful friends and my family. You're all the best and I couldn't have done this without you.

I would like to thank my Street Team - The Z Team. Ladies, you're the best an Author can ask for.

Sione, my fabulous editor, thank you for keeping with me, keeping me going, and for putting up with me. This last year has been amazing and I can't thank you enough.

Rachel and Barb - Thank you for putting up with me, and for bring my biggest fans.

And to my AMAZING FANS! I couldn't do this without you!

Find More Zoey

On Twitter: www.twitter.com/ZoeyDerrick
On Facebook: www.facebook.com/Zoey.Derrick.1 -
Personal
www.facebook.com/Zoey.Derrick (Author)
On Her Website: www.ZoeyDerrick.com
Email Her: Zoey@ZoeyDerrick.com
Amazon Author Page: Find it Here

Other Works By Zoey Derrick

Finding Love's Wings

CAMERON ENDERS seems to have it all: a brand new
condo in a city she loves, a top executive position at an
international entertainment firm, an insane amount of
money, and a gorgeous boyfriend. But when Cami
catches the boyfriend in the act with another woman, it
triggers all the anguish from years of neglect by her
parents, and she realizes she never learned how to love
or be loved. Cami flees to the remote tropical island of

Tarah, but she can't avoid facing her problems any longer when she meets the man of her fantasies...

TRISTAN MICHAELS, one of Hollywood's hottest new stars, has come to Tarah to ride out a storm. His girlfriend of five years has been caught on camera cheating, and she's determined to make Tristan stop the story from breaking. But Tristan's done cleaning up her messes. He needs to escape all things Hollywood for a while--and especially the firm that represents him--until the whole thing blows over. What he doesn't count on is meeting an irresistibly beautiful woman, a woman who just so happens to be the CEO of the firm he's trying to avoid.

Can Tristan and Cami help each other learn to trust and love again, or will their histories of betrayal tear them apart?

This story contains Tattoos, Piercings, a Hot Movie Star and a Sexy Heroine. No rich guy poor girl story here, just a story of what it's like to learn to love.

The Struggle
27 writers. 29 original stories and poems. A single theme:
The Struggle.

Proceeds from the sale of this anthology will go to helping writers in need.

From horror and humor to love and loss, each tale reflects the struggles we all have to face – in life, and within ourselves. They are as varied as the array of talent who united to create them, spinning the threads of storytelling together to weave an extraordinary anthology unlike any other.

The Struggle features works by Delilah S. Dawson, Michael Birchmore, Bobby Salomons, Sue Birchmore, James R. Tuck, Corey Seeley, Sheila Hall, Lily Luchesi, Karina Cooper, Mari Wells, Andrea Wheeler, Sarah Broadley, J. Luis Licea, Zoey Derrick, Aly Morlock, Casey Harris-Parks, Samantha Lee, Trevor Neale, J. Elizabeth Hill, Romantic Dominant, J. Hewitt, Christopher Liccardi, Caroline Rainbow, Gabi Daniels, Peter Davis-Parker, and Rick Austin.

About Zoey

Amazon Best Selling Angels, Demons & Devils and
Paranormal Author of Give Me Reason - The Reason
Series Book One comes from Glendale, Arizona. Zoey,
was a mortgage underwriter by day and is now a
paranormal, romance and erotica novelist full-time. She
writes stories as hot as the desert sun itself. It is this
passion that drips off of her work, bringing excitement to
anyone who enjoys a good and sensual love story.

Not only does she aim to take her readers on an erotic
dance that lasts the night, it allows her to empty her mind
of stories we all wish were true.
Her stories are hopeful yet true to life, skillfully avoiding
melodrama and the unrealistic, bringing her gripping
Erotica only closer to the heart of those that dare dipping
into it.

The intimacy of her fantasies that she shares with her
readers is thrilling and encouraging, climactic yet full of
suspense. She is a loving mistress, up for anything, of
which any reader is doomed to return to again and again.

www.ingramcontent.com/pod-product-compliance
Lightning Source LLC
Chambersburg PA
CBHW050934120626
46552CB00001B/204